Kennedy spoke in a tone of voice only a notch or two above normal when he said, "Mister, let go of that carbine! Don't turn, and don't try to duck away—just let go of the Winchester!"

The startled outlaw did turn. He twisted violently from the waist to look back. Bart held his breath, expecting Kennedy to shoot. Instead the town marshal again called upon the startled outlaw to drop his weapon. The outlaw did not obey, and somewhere south of him a man's quick, alarmed voice called out. "What the hell is it? What's out there, Slim?"

Slim ignored the questions. He stared steadily at Kennedy and Bart for the better part of five seconds, then tightened his body and in a blur of speed, threw himself sideways as Kennedy fired . . .

THE HORSEMAN

Lauran Paine

FAWCETT GOLD MEDAL • NEW YORK

CHAPTER 1

Out of the Storm

It was one of those dismal gray days before a rain when the sky had a pewter overcast, the air was still, and although visibility was excellent and a man could see as far as Wild Horse Mesa, about thirty miles north, the total stillness was a warning of the storm to come.

To the weather-tanned man standing in front of his sod-roofed log barn, all the signs were abundantly evident: It was going to rain like a fat cow peeing off a flat rock. His earlier intention to saddle up and go hunt for his brood mares dwindled as he watched the sky, the rolling grassland beyond his yard, and the motionless trees over by his log house and outbuildings.

Nothing moved; it was as though everything in sight for as far as he could see was holding its breath, waiting for the lead-bellied clouds to open up.

He was in his late thirties, scarred and calloused from manual labor. There was a sprinkling of premature gray at his temples and a direct, calculating hardness to his gaze.

He had homesteaded his claim four years ago, had proved up on it, had worked long summer days to get his buildings completed before winter cold drove him indoors. Being sixty miles from a town—a place called Holtville—was both a curse and a blessing. He was rarely intruded upon, which satisfied him, but when he needed supplies, it was a long drive over and back in his old Green River wagon. Otherwise, he had no complaints. In four years he had built up a nice herd of horses, twenty-seven brood mares, and a government remount stallion.

He had broken and sold a lot of nice colts over the past couple of years. His reputation as an honest horse rancher had reached even farther than Holtville.

Twice he'd had to go up to Wild Horse Mesa and bring back horses. The first time because some wild stallion had come down to his grassland range, rounded up six of his open mares, and had choused them back atop the mesa in a dead run. The second time the situation had been reversed, his remount stallion, half Morgan and half Texas quarter-running horse, had picked up the scent of open mares atop the mesa and had gone up to bring back ten head.

Both times the thieving stallions had managed their foray without encountering each other, otherwise there would have been a battle that could have left them both badly hurt, or perhaps could have left one of them dead. That was why Templeton was out front of his barn balancing his desire to know where his mares were against the impending downpour—he did not want his remount horse all cut to hell by some inbred wild stallion whose ears both came out the same hole.

If he lost his stallion, he would still have a colt crop between eleven and twelve months hence, which would be next spring, but since Bart Templeton did not start colts until they were three years old, the loss of his seed horse would disrupt his breeding and starting schedules. Although in a good year while he made top wages, enough money to satisfy his needs, support his ranch-development program, and pay on the note at the Holtville bank, he would be out of the horse-ranching business within a couple of years if he lost Big Ben, the remount studhorse.

He leaned on the hitch-rack in front of the barn, eyeing that menacing sky and listening to the hush that was like a blanket.

His range ran to within ten miles of Wild Horse Mesa to the north. To the south, east, and west it was rolling country with occasional pockets of trees. The creek running behind his log house also came from the north, following an ancient course as crooked as a dog's hind leg. This was good livestock country. Three miles east was the Holbrook cattle outfit, one of the largest in the territory. To the west was woodland about six miles distant. That was where he had snaked back the logs for his buildings. It had been a two-day haul going out there, dropping the trees, limbing and trimming them, then skidding them to the yard.

As John Holbrook had said after waiting out the homesteader, expecting him to go belly-up as most of them did, Bart Templeton was bred out of the old school; he worked long hours, and very hard. He would wring a living from that land of his if anyone could.

And, by the third year, old John also said that if a man had to have a close neighbor he could do no better than to have one like Templeton.

But they were no more than nodding acquaintances. John Holbrook was moneyed and tough. He had come into the Blue Basin country as a young man with half a hundred razorback, wicked-horned Texas cattle. Half a century later Holbrook cattle were bred-up, beefy animals, and while old John's Indian wife had died eleven years earlier, his daughter Nan—with skin the color of new cream, jet black hair, and eyes—did most of the riding old John could no longer do. His back confined him to wagons or buggies.

He had an obsidian bird-arrow embedded in a lumbar vertebra. Doctors in Denver had told him they could remove it but the chances of the operation leaving him unable to walk were very great.

John Holbrook had come home, bought a new buggy, and given his daughter more and more authority. He also increased his drinking, but less out of frustration than because of almost constant pain.

The last time Bart Templeton had seen him, John had a jug on the floorboard of his top-buggy. That had been the previous autumn when Bart had brought back a band of Holbrook cattle that had strayed onto Templeton grass.

John and Nan had been at their marking ground with the riding crew. They had thanked Bart for driving in the cattle and old John had offered him the jug. Bart had taken a couple of swallows, although it was not even midday, and despite his aversion to straight whiskey. Then he had returned home, where he had three big colts in the corrals out behind the barn awaiting their turns at being sacked-out and rigged with breaking hackamores.

Bart had three green colts in the corrals out back now, and having decided not to ride in search of the mares, he entered the barn, took down three hackamores with thick cotton reins, and stepped through the barn's rear doorless opening—and a big, fat raindrop struck his cheek.

He stopped and raised his face. Another fat raindrop struck his forehead. At his feet other raindrops hit the ground sending up tiny explosions of dust.

He considered the wary colts who were watching his every move. The raindrops continued to fall; Bart returned to the barn, draped the breaking hackamores from their pegs, and went out front again. From his yard looking north and east, he saw that the increasing force of the downpour added a gray veil to the distances. The air began to smell clean, and behind him, his sod-roofed barn was beginning to darken from moisture.

Somewhere to the north, but also westerly behind his barn, he heard a man shout. For a moment he continued to lean on the tie rack; there was no one living in that direction. As he straightened up to walk down through the barn again he thought in terms of grub-line saddle-tramps, or possibly pothunters on their way to Holtville with deer or elk carcasses on pack animals.

In the rain-dimmed near-distance he saw two riders, not just the one he had expected. They were riding about fifteen feet apart and were leading a horse between them, each man with his lariat leading from the led animal to a saddle horn. The only horses people led like that were outlaw horses it was necessary to cross-lead in order to prevent the horse from lunging and attacking one rider or the other.

The men were wearing heavy rain-soaked coats, disreputable old hats, were unshaven and unkempt-appearing, and the horse they had between them had one eye swollen closed and caked blood on his mouth and nostrils. He was tucked up, skinned from having been thrown a couple of times to take the fight out of him, and now as he plodded along with his head down and his one good eye dully fixed upon the man in the barn doorway, he had a fit of coughing, which moved his captors to swear and yank savagely on their lead-ropes.

Bart moved away from the barn's protection and opened a corral gate.

As the strangers dragged their battered wild horse inside, then forced him against the log stringers in order to get their ropes off him, one of them, a dark, grinning man built like a bear, looked over and spoke above the sound of the storm. "Sure grateful we seen this place. We're new in this country and was beginnin' to believe we'd never find shelter."

They rode good horses. Bart noticed this as they led them out, waited for him to close and bar the gate, then took their horses inside the barn to be off-saddled. Because of the sod roof, it was quiet inside the barn. The bear-built dark man shucked a glove, pushed out a thick hand, and smiled as he said, "Right obliged for your hospitality, friend. My name is Jasper Perry and that there is my brother, Jim Perry."

Templeton acknowledged the introduction and asked about the big bay horse.

The darker of the brothers continued to smile as he replied. "We come from Wyoming, headin' south so's we won't have to put in no more cold winters. Come due south through the mountains. Come out atop that big mesa up yonder day before yestiddy. Seen horse sign so we scouted a little. That bay horse was in a box canyon with about twenty mares and some colts. We sized things up and me bein' the best roper, Jim come down the wall of the box canyon and spooked 'em toward the open end where I was waitin' on my horse. Roped him neat as a whistle when he come chargin' out of there with his band. Mister, that horse put up a fight a man'd have to see to believe. I had m'hands full until Jim come along and got his rope on the horse too. Even then he fought like a tiger, rearing, striking, trying to lunge and bite. Even threw himself a few times. I thought for a while we'd have to shoot him just to get our ropes back. Instead, we tripped him. Every time he'd show fight we'd dump him. That's how he hurt his eye and bloodied his muzzle. . . . Two days of fightin' him before he'd lead, and two more days gettin' down this far with him."

Bart nodded. He'd caught his share of mustangs, but this was a large horse, a stallion, not more than maybe five or six years old. He said, "What're you going to do with him?"

Jasper Perry's grin widened as he faced Bart. "We're goin' to sell him to you, friend. Six dollars cash on the barrel head."

Jim Perry, who was fairer and slightly taller than his brother, spoke up. "Where is the nearest town?" When Bart told him, he sighed, glanced at his brother, and wagged his head. "We're not draggin' that blasted horse any sixty miles, Jasper. If this gent don't want him I'll take him out a ways and shoot him."

Bart said, "Three dollars."

Jim opened his mouth to speak, but Jasper cut in first. "Four and you got yourself a fine big wild horse. Four dollars, supper tonight, the dry barn to sleep in, and he's yours."

Bart dug in a trouser pocket, brought forth four silver cartwheels, which he handed to Jasper Perry, then helped them hang their saddles and blankets and bridles, stall their horses, pitch some timothy hay into their mangers from the loft, then he led them across the soggy yard to the log house. He needed that battered, probably half-blind big wild horse like he needed a case of the plague, but he did not doubt for one moment that they would do as Jim had said—lead him away in the morning and shoot him on the range somewhere. The horse didn't deserve that; all he'd been trying to do was regain his freedom the only way any stallion knew to do it—by fighting tooth and hoof as hard and as long as he could.

CHAPTER 2

A Visitor

It was drizzling when the Perry brothers rode out of the yard in the direction of Holtville, their clothes dry, their bellies full, and four dollars richer.

Bart watched them from in front of the barn, then went out back to fork-feed to the wild horse. The animal ate, but not with enthusiasm. His swollen eye looked worse. He had cuts and scratches that needed attention, but no one in his right mind would try to corner that big bay horse to doctor him.

There was a large fir-log snubbing post in the center of the corral, but Bart did not have the heart to rope and snub the wild stallion; he'd had about all the abuse he could handle.

After feeding the three colts in the adjoining corral, Bart studied the sky. There was no break in the leaden overcast, which meant that the storm was not going to let up.

At least not for some time, perhaps not today and maybe not even tomorrow. He went back to the house and cleaned up the breakfast dishes, then got busy doing something he only did when he could not do much else—he cleaned house.

It was not a chore he cared about. He only used two rooms—one of the two bedrooms and the kitchen—so the rest of the house accumulated dust rather than dirt.

By midday the drizzle was beginning to ease up. As was customary under these circumstances, there was a wet ground-fog sifting in. When Bart went out to fill the kitchen woodbox, he glanced out across the yard and saw horses. His remount studhorse, Big Ben, was bringing in his harem.

Bart went to the front porch under the overhang to watch. Big Ben detected the smell of the other stallion and threw up his head, began to cakewalk a little, and bowed his neck. The mares were only casually interested in the corralled animal, but Big Ben, who was not quite as tall but thicker than the wild horse and about the same shade of bay color, took them around behind the barn toward the network of pole corrals.

Ben went straight up to the corral fence and bellowed a challenge. The wild horse peered from his one good eye and forgetting his aches and pains, cakewalked to the same side of the corral to whistle, duck his head a few times, and snort.

The mares watched, mostly in order to know when to herd their colts away if a fight started. But there was no fight; the stallions tried to bite each other's necks across the corral poles. They pawed and reared, whistled and bellowed a lot, but that was a very strong pole fence between them.

Bart went to the woodshed, got an armload, and returned to the house. It was not cold out, but it was damp and chilly, so he made a pot of fresh coffee. While waiting for it to boil, he returned to the front veranda. But Big Ben had taken his mares away, nipping rumps to keep them heading west. He had no intention of having the wild horse get loose to steal part of his harem.

Bart smiled, eyed his soggy world, and the fading gray above, and went out back to lean on the corral, watching the four-dollar big bay studhorse. The horse looked back from the opposite side of the corral. Rain had washed most of the caked blood off, but the eye that was swollen closed gave the horse's head a lopsided appearance. Bart shook his head. It was necessary to rough up unbroke and wild horses, but not to the extent this horse had been roughed up.

He would alter him, of course. No one needed two stallions on one range. He was a tad over the age when Bart usually castrated studs. He looked to be maybe five years old. Bart usually altered them at two or three.

He was tall, close to sixteen hands, and he was rangy and muscular. Someday he would make someone a powerful saddle animal. Providing, of course, he was not blind in that injured eye.

The drizzle stopped, the ground-fog thickened, and Bart returned to the house for hot coffee.

By late afternoon the sky was beginning to clear. The following morning sunlight broke over the soggy range causing steam to rise. By ten o'clock there was warmth, so he went back to the corrals to work with the three green colts. They were not far enough along to ride, which was just as well, because the ground was like grease. He spent the balance of the day working the colts from the ground, which was where two-thirds of the breaking process was accomplished anyway.

In the afternoon the sun had begun its healing process. By then he had ground-driven two of the big colts and had pretty well got the third one accustomed to having a man close to him.

He spent an hour with the wild horse. A horse that had been abused required more attention than green colts who had had no previous contact with human beings. He was unable to get very close, but at least the wild horse did not try to climb out of the corral; he kept moving away, sidling left and right, his one good eye fixed upon the two-legged creature in the corral with him. The only time he showed any sign of acceptance was when Bart brought him a forkful of timothy hay from the barn, and stood beside it until the wild horse sidled up to snatch a mouthful before whirling away. He talked to the horse; he talked to all horses, even when he was riding them. The big bay's ears moved each time the man spoke to him, and his one good eye warily watched. He came back to snatch several more mouthfuls of hay and wheel away before he eventually decided the stationary man was not going to move clear of the hay nor strike him with the pitchfork. Then he minced up and dropped his head to eat while keeping his good eye fixed upon the man. The distance between them was about six feet. It wasn't much, but Bart knew it was a start. Maybe the big bay wouldn't be as difficult to handle as he had originally seemed.

Bart did not need the wild horse. He did not even want him, especially since he was a stallion, but to a horse-breaker of considerable experience the big bay represented a challenge, and that was the key to the personality of all horsebreakers.

After supper he bedded down early, which was his custom, because he rolled out early.

By the afternoon of the fifth day he could not put a hand on the big bay, but he could get right up beside him without being lunged at. Bart represented hay to the wild horse. Hay and quiet conversation. By the seventh day the swelling had gone down considerably; the injured eye was visible through puffy flesh. It focused well and was a little bloodshot, but evidently it had not been irreversibly damaged.

That seventh day Bart saddled a gentle horse and went west in search of Big Ben and his mares. He left early and returned in midafternoon after locating the horses in a bosque of white oaks about four miles southwest of his yard. As he was returning he saw a saddle animal tied out front of the barn, and someone standing beside the round corral looking in at his wild horse.

He did not have any neighbors closer than the Holbrooks. When he loped into the yard and the visitor turned to watch him swing off and tie up, he did not recognize Nan Holbrook. She waited for him beside the corral. When he got back there, she said, "Where did you get him?" and jutted her jaw in the direction of the wild horse.

He told her the entire story from the beginning and when he had finished, she said, "I'll give you a profit, Bart. Three times in cash what you paid for him."

He shoved a foot atop the bottommost corral stringer, gazing at the big horse. "I don't think so, Nan. What would you do with him? He'd kill you."

"No, he wouldn't. I'd turn him over to Simon Butler, our horsebreaker on the ranch."

Bart smiled without facing her. He knew Simon Butler; he could break green colts, but this horse was something altogether different. "He's a stallion, and he's been hurt a lot. He'll fight. That's all he knows how to do."

She leaned beside him, also gazing in at the bay horse. "What happened to his head?"

"They threw him. Maybe they also used a tree limb on him. It's a lot better than it was a week ago. The eye's all right."

"Will he let you touch it?"

"Yes. But he's spooky about it. He let me put grease on the scratches and cuts, though."

"How old is he, Bart?"

"Five, by his mouth." As he said this, he turned to study her profile. She was a beautiful woman and did not appear to realize it. "What are you doing this far from Holbrook range?"

She dismissed his question by saying, "That was a good rain, but it confines a person to the yard."

He accepted her oblique reply and returned his attention to the bay stallion. "I'll tell you what I'll do: After I break him and have put a lot of sweaty saddle blankets under him,

I'll ride over, and if you still want him, we'll work something out." He turned his attention to the three green colts, to one in particular, a flashy chestnut sorrel with a flaxen mane and tail. He had been altered, was muscled-up, and had a good set of dark eyes in a handsome head. "There's one that when you rode him through Holtville folks would turn to look."

She studied the horse, slowly nodded in agreement, but returned her gaze to the big bay. "Not in the same class, Bart. Someday this one will make a top-notch using horse."

He could not fault that, so he muttered, "Someday." Then, changing the subject, he turned to her and asked, "How's your pa?"

A cloud passed across her face. "I wish he'd have the operation."

"And maybe never walk again?"

"There are worse things."

"Name one."

"Drinking yourself to death."

He leaned on the corral, looking away from her. "I guess so."

Her tone changed, lightened a little. "Have you been over to Holtville lately?"

He shook his head.

"The railroad company is building shipping corrals."

He thought about that before saying, "They must figure to bring the tracks in."

She nodded. "They're working north from Gardnerville. The folks in Holtville are excited. By next summer they'll have a railroad siding. It will bring business. Holtville will grow."

Bart dryly said, "Yeah. And how does your pa like that idea?"

"Not very well. He says it'll also bring homesteaders and riffraff."

Bart shifted position a little. He had been a rangeman all

his mature life. He had been top-hand for some large cow outfits, and although he had descended to the level of a squatter by homesteading his land, he knew exactly how large cattlemen like her father felt about homesteaders. He also knew that to some extent their attitude was justified.

"It'll be a while, Nan. And Blue Basin is a big country. Anyway, if stockmen have got deeds to their ranges, they don't have much to worry about."

She raised a gloved hand to push back a heavy coil of jet-black hair that had fallen across her forehead. "It's change," she said to him. "Nothing is very different in Blue Basin from how it was when my father came here half a century ago. They don't like change. People like my father are against newcomers on general principles." She caught her lower lip between her teeth and released it, looking at him. "Not you. My father likes you. So do I." She straightened up a little, and while eyeing the wild horse, changed the direction of their conversation. "Two men dynamited the vault at the bank up in Stillwater. Did you hear about that?"

He hadn't. He was usually the last to hear things like this because he rarely made the trip to town. "No. Did they get much money?"

"All of it. Eleven thousand dollars. As they ran out to their horses a barman whose building adjoined the bank and who was nearly knocked flat by the explosion, ran out into the roadway with a rifle. He shot one of them as they were racing out of town."

"Killed him?"

"Yes. But he didn't have the money. That was two weeks ago. Since then, there have been possemen from Stillwater and also from Holtville combing the country in between."

Bart said, "That'd be about a hundred miles of mountains, if he kept coming south and stayed clear of the stageroad."

Nan Holbrook watched the bay horse lower his head and

raise a hind hoof to scratch behind his ear. "There is a two thousand dollar reward. One of our riders wanted to take time off and go manhunting. My father told him that if he left, he needn't return."

Bart shrugged. In two weeks a desperate man, providing he was well mounted, could have passed through the Blue Basin country almost any night, and by this time be two-thirds of the way to the Mexican border. He turned his head. "Would you like some coffee?"

She hung fire, but only very briefly, before accepting the offer, and as they turned away from the corral, she fell in beside him. Even though her mother had been Indian, Nan's complexion was fairer than that of the man she was walking with.

As they were nearing the house, he said, "For two thousand dollars someone will catch up to him even down in Mexico."

It was a very large bounty, considering the amount of money the outlaw had gotten away with. Ordinarily rewards did not exceed five hundred dollars, even for murderers.

CHAPTER 3

The Days of Summer

Two days after Nan Holbrook's visit Bart was riding the northwest range, up where his horses usually went when the summer heat made them seek shade, and along the base of the rough mountainous country with its perpetual forest-gloom; he found them in a bosquet of white oaks where Willow Creek left the uplands to begin its meandering course down across the grassland. This was the same watercourse that bisected his land and made a dogleg bend behind his house.

The horses were accustomed to being scouted up by their owner. Even Big Ben simply watched his approach without excitement.

There were two new colts, wobbly-legged with bulging foreheads and baby hair where their manes would be later on. He halted in tree-shade, counted the mares, then the colts. Some were six or eight months old. Almost old enough to be weaned, but that was up to their mothers.

The animals looked good; even the wet mares were slick. The colts were sassy-fat, and when he went closer, several of them threw up their heads and tails and ran in big circles. Bart laughed at them, their mothers watched all this with no great concern, and when the running was finished, the colts came breathlessly back to the band.

He dismounted and approached Big Ben. The muscular bay stallion put his head down to get his forehead scratched, during which process he stood hip-shot with both eyes half closed. Big Ben was by nature a placid, friendly animal. He would fight, and he would keep his mares in line, but he was something unusual in a range horse—he liked two-legged creatures.

Bart led his saddle animal to the creek to tank up, and got belly-down among the willows and rank grass also to drink. As he was raising up, his eyes at about knee-level of his horse, he saw smoke. It was distant and it was closer to the lift of mountains north of the foothills than it was to the foothills where there was much less timber, but it was unmistakably smoke and it was also unmistakably on his deeded land.

He stood up and leaned across the saddle-seat, studying it as his saddle animal cropped grass.

The smoke was not heavy; it arose in the still summer midday like rope, and had it not been silhouetted by the darker uplands, he might not have noticed it.

It was the wrong time of year for trappers to be in the mountains and the smoke was too low down for it to be the cooking fire of pothunters. He guessed it might be the fire of mustangers. It was in the direction of Wild Horse Mesa.

There was an old army wagon road over there. It had not been in use for twenty years, not since the last horse soldiers had routed the last of the redskin holdouts from pockets of resistance in the Blue Mountains.

He squinted at the sun to estimate how much daylight he had left, then he mounted his horse and headed in the direction of the smoke.

Behind him, Big Ben had decided that after the interruption of his siesta by the rider, it was time for his mares to leave the creek and go out to graze. He began herding them southwest away from the shade.

The sun was still high when Bart reached the badly eroded wagon road and turned east along it with the thin gray spindrift of a cooking fire a mile or two on eastward. There were washouts in the roadbed, which required him to skirt up into the trees to avoid them, and because of this he was hidden from view part of the time.

When he could smell the smoke, inherent caution made him remain north of the old road up through the trees until he topped out on a wind-scourged, gravelly ridge with an excellent view in three directions.

Below him and about a half mile eastward on the old road was a faded wagon with slack canvas draped over ash bows. The tongue was on the ground. There were two sets of chain harness hanging from the front wheels, and about fifteen feet from the wagon was a stone ring to contain the fire that was sending up the streamer of smoke. The fire had been banked; someone had scuffed ash and soil over it to dampen the flames. It was this covering that was making the smoke.

Three horses were grazing southward of the camp. Two were big twelve-hundred-pound team horses. The third animal was a worn-down, lean saddle horse.

Bart dismounted to hunker in front of his horse, studying the camp. As he watched, a man climbed down over the tailgate with a wooden bucket in his hand. Even from the distance separating them, Bart could see the faded, patched condition of the man's trousers and shirt. He was rawboned and neither young nor old. His hair was too long and his heavy-boned, wide shoulders were stooped. His general appearance was of weariness.

Bart waited until the man disappeared up through the trees in search of water before getting on his horse and moving down toward the roadbed.

He was within about three hundred feet of the camp when

the man came back out of the timber carrying a bucket that was obviously full. They saw each other at about the same time and the rawboned man paused a moment, then lengthened his stride as though he wanted to reach the wagon before Bart did.

Without hurrying Bart rode on up. The rawboned man had already disappeared inside the old wagon when Bart swung to the ground beside the stone ring and looked around. There were some drying strips of what appeared to be bed-sheeting hanging from a rope that had been stretched from a rear wheel of the wagon to a nearby sapling, and there were some cast-iron cooking pots beside the stone ring.

Bart was tying his horse to the near side-front wheel when a second man slid down over the tailgate. This man was older and thicker. He wore an ivory-handled six-gun and when he faced Bart, he neither nodded nor spoke, just stood beside the wagon taking Bart's measure.

Instinct told Bart to be very careful. It also told him that although this was obviously a settler wagon and at least the first man he had seen was probably a homesteader, this older man with the ivory-handled six-gun on his right side was not. He nodded, straightened around as he began removing his riding gloves, and said, "Good morning. I saw your fire from out a ways. Is anything wrong?"

The older man had a square jaw and stone-steady gray eyes in a tanned, rather handsome face. He could have been forty or fifty, and he was sturdily put up. He did not offer an immediate reply, not until the second man came out of the wagon to join him. There was a great contrast between them. The younger man was taller and had deeply etched worry lines in his face as he faced Bart; the older one was much heavier, appeared expressionless and watchful. Eventually he said, "There is a little trouble, yes. Who are you?"

"Bart Templeton. I run horses hereabouts. In fact, you're camped on my range."

The younger man said, "I'm Emory Wilton. He's Tom Jones. My wife's inside. We had to stop here because she went into labor. The baby wasn't comin' right and I didn't know what to do. Mr. Jones came along. He's been through this before. He delivered the baby and for three days he's been doctoring my wife."

Bart considered Tom Jones and for some unfathomable reason he thought of the outlaw who had escaped after robbing the bank a hundred miles north through the mountains up at Stillwater. Nan had offered no description but two things about Tom Jones were obvious. One was that he did not belong among meandering homesteaders. The other thing was that while ivory-handled six-guns were not a rarity, ordinary range-riders did not wear them because they could not afford them.

Whoever Tom Jones was, there was something about him that made him appear to be someone whose normal occupation was not delivering babies and tending their mothers. He just stood there looking steadily at Bart without opening his mouth.

Bart said, "How is your wife now, Mr. Wilton?"

Wilton's answer was noncommittal. "She seems better today. At least the bleeding has stopped. But she's awful weak, Mr. Templeton."

Bart had been about to suggest harnessing the team and heading for Holtville, where there was a widely respected midwife, but if the woman had been hemorrhaging and was weak, that long drive over uneven terrain might be worse for her than remaining where she was. He leaned against the wagon wheel. "There is a town about seventy miles or so southeast of here. There's a lady lives down there who's been delivering babies in the Blue Basin country since long before I came here." He paused a moment, then said,

"Maybe I could ride down and get her to come back with me."

Wilton looked inquiringly at the older man standing beside him, and Tom Jones finally spoke, addressing Bart. "It won't be necessary. Besides that, it'd most likely cost a fortune. You can't get people to do things like that without paying them. Mr. Wilton here and his wife are home-steaders from Kansas on their way out to the Oregon country to take up land and go to farming. They don't have much, Mr. Templeton. It'd suit them best if you wouldn't object to them camping on your land until Missus Wilton is able to travel again. I think they'd take that real kindly."

Emory Wilton solemnly moved his head up and down. "We would for a fact," he told Bart. "Now that Emily's on the mend, if I didn't have to move her for a spell, Mr. Templeton . . ."

Bart smiled. "Stay as long as you want." He turned to free his reins from the wagon wheels. "Anything else I can do?"

Tom Jones said, "Where is your ranch?"

Bart pointed. "Yonder about ten or twelve miles."

"You're quite a distance from town."

"About sixty miles. I go over there with a wagon about three times a year for supplies."

Tom Jones seemed to be turning this over in his mind as he watched Bart snug up the cinch before mounting. As Bart was turning his horse, the older man spoke again. "It'd be a day's ride up and back for you, Mr. Templeton, but if you had reason to come to your north range two or three days from now to see how Missus Wilton is coming along, I'm sure these folks would be right grateful to you."

Again the rawboned young man bobbed his head up and down.

Bart sat in the saddle gazing at them. His impression of Wilton was that he was exactly what he seemed to be; a wandering farmer in search of land to settle on. Tom Jones, on the other hand, appeared to be a wary individual without much warmth, even though he evidently had lingered with the homesteaders long enough to help the woman recover from a trying childbirth. He seemed to be a man it would be hard to know; there was something different, almost challenging, about him.

Bart agreed to ride up to the camp again in a few days and left the men standing there watching him ride back the way he had come.

It was a long ride back to the yard, but he'd had an encounter with strangers that kept his mind occupied all the way. Although there were dark shadows when he entered the yard and swung off in front of the barn, he cared for his mount and then went out back to fork-feed to the corralled horses. Bart spent a half hour in the corral with the bay stallion.

By now they had a working understanding of each other and with nearly all the swelling gone from the stallion's eye, he watched everything the man did with unimpaired vision.

He allowed himself to be greased, to be patted on the neck, and he did not whirl away when Bart made a close inspection of his eye.

Bart went inside and ate supper by lamplight. While he was eating, he decided he would alter the bay horse in a day or two. But tomorrow he would sack him out and fit him for a breaking hackamore, because the same day he castrated the bay horse, he intended to saddle him and ride him. He would not take the horse as far north as the wagon-camp, but he would put a few miles under him before the horse recovered his strength from being altered.

The following morning there were cloud-galleons of enormous size drifting lazily down from the north, and while they probably presaged more rain, it was equally as possible that the rain would not arrive for several days.

He sacked out the stallion, using a saddle blanket. He

encountered wariness but no combativeness. He also fitted a hackamore, and this the bay horse stood for with deceptive calm. Only his eyes showed that he was considering everything the man did from the standpoint of an iron resolve not to allow the man too much familiarity.

In the afternoon Bart rode the chestnut gelding with the flaxen mane and tail. He poneyed him in the round corral for an hour. The chestnut horse was tractable, but one hour a day was enough; any more made some horses sulk, which was something to be avoided. An hour a day was enough for a man too.

By evening he was tired and sweaty, so he took a chunk of lye soap and a towel to the creek behind the house and had an allover bath. Dressed in clean clothing, he returned to the house for supper. He felt much better after bathing and eating. He even filled a cup with half water and half whiskey from the jug he kept in a kitchen cupboard, and went down to lean on the corral stringers as he sipped his drink, watching the horses, talking to them, speculating on what was going to happen the first time he got onto the back of the wild horse.

The next day those huge white cloud banks had drifted so far west he could no longer see them, and there did not appear to be any more like them over the far horizon.

He rode the chestnut horse out of the yard, squaw-reining him and using gentle knee pressure to cover three miles out and three miles back. For the flashy chestnut horse that was his first sweaty saddle blanket.

Bart spent the afternoon with lariats, a very sharp knife, the snubbing post, and the bay stallion. When he was finished, the bay horse had become a gelding, and whatever slight faith he had begun to feel in the man was gone. Bart would have to start over—not completely, but to a considerable extent he would have to regain the horse's trust.

What the horse had learned so far he would not forget, but his consideration of the man who had castrated him would now include a measure of fear. It would be leavened with the passage of time, but it would never leave him again as long as he lived. He would do what two-legged creatures required of him, and as time passed he would do it willingly, but for the rest of his life there would be a thin vein of fear toward all human beings.

CHAPTER 4

A Day to Remember

When a man weighed about a hundred and seventy pounds and the horse he intended to break weighed a thousand pounds, the secret of success for the man was to take every advantage.

There was another factor: When a horse was altered, he had to be made to move, to exercise, or his hind legs would stock up, would swell, and that would further inhibit him from wanting to move. The result could be permanent damage.

Not all horsebreakers took this kind of an advantage of a green horse, but Bart Templeton did because not only was the horse forced to exercise so he would not stock up, but a freshly altered horse was sore in the body and was therefore demoralized in the head. He might want to buck and fight, but instinct would keep him from doing it because fighting would increase his pain.

Bart rigged out the bay horse, left the corral gate open, mounted him inside, and kneed him out through the gate at a humped-up, painful walk. The bay horse walked with a shortened gait, but the battle he would otherwise surely have put up did not come.

Bart rode him a mile out and a mile back. He then sluiced the blood off his hocks and left him saddled and tied.

Later in the afternoon he rode him again. This time the horse was stiffer because he had been standing, but because he was ridden over the exact same route out and back, he went along without much fuss.

It was dusk when he pulled the rigging off, sluiced the blood off again, and left the horse in his corral with a big bait of hay.

He spent what daylight remained riding the chestnut horse, who understood what squaw-reining meant by now, and who did not even break nor shy violently when a brush rabbit sprang out of some undergrowth as he walked past. Bart patted his neck and talked to him. This one, he knew, was going to be one of those horses it pleasured a man to handle, and that made him think of Nan Holbrook. A beautiful woman riding a handsome horse was something to behold. He was off-saddling the chestnut when it occurred to him that if he rode the chestnut over to the Holbrook yard the next day she would have an opportunity to appreciate the kind of animal this was.

But he did not do it because in the morning the bay horse was beginning to stock up when he went out to pitch feed. The bay horse was also beginning to feel less pain and eyed Bart with more spirit than he had showed the previous two days.

Bart saddled him, turned him several times, always toward himself so that when he toed in to spring up, the turning motion of the horse would put him in the saddle without effort.

Then he kneed the horse out through the gate. For a mile they went over the same trail they had used two previous times. The bay walked along with no humping up for a change, but he still had a foreshortened step.

Bart turned and started back. The bay horse raised his head. Bart did not see Big Ben and his harem because he had been concentrating on the horse he was straddling. But when Big Ben caught the scent of the bay horse and whistled a fighting challenge, Bart swung his head at the same moment the remount stallion left his band and started in a loose lope for Bart and the bay horse.

The unexpected but predictable crisis made Bart's mind perfectly clear. Even if he tried to make the bay horse lope toward the yard Big Ben would follow, and because the wild horse was not yet able to extend himself in a dead run, Big Ben would overtake them and attack.

Big Ben halted a hundred or so yards out, dropped his head as he pawed, then flung his head up, and bellowed a fighting call.

The wild horse refused to respond to the hackamore knot along his jawbones near his chin and swung to face the remount stallion. This was something the bay horse knew by heart—how to fight. All his mature life he had been fighting off challenges by other stallions to his mares. Bart was convinced that in a head-on battle the horse he was riding would whip Big Ben, and although Bart had been in almost every conceivable crisis with horses he was breaking, he had never before been on the back of one in a stud-fight.

He was not wearing his gun and shellbelt, otherwise he might have risked a shot to make Big Ben turn away. Even though if he had been wearing his gun and had fired it from the back of the big bay horse, there would have been a very good possibility that before the echoes died he would be riding a runaway animal.

A lot of men had been killed by runaways.

He yelled at Big Ben but might as well have yelled at a stone wall. Ben was pawing again. Bart knew that this time he would not stop when he charged.

The big wild horse kept his head toward the remount horse. He stopped stone-still and refused to respond to Bart's knee and heel pressure. The big bay knew what was coming and had positioned himself for it, facing his adversary.

When the charge started, Bart gripped leather with both legs. The distant mares and colts watched idly.

At the very last moment, when Bart could see the fiery brilliance of Big Ben's eyes less than twenty feet away, the big wild horse whirled, nearly losing Bart. Ben reared high to come down against the other horse's rump, but the big bay horse lashed out with both hind legs, again nearly flinging Bart from the saddle.

Bart heard both hooves strike Ben. The sound was similar to that made by someone striking a bag of flour with a heavy club. With both legs and hands occupied with keeping himself from being flung off, Bart twisted to look back. The big horse's timing had been perfect. One hoof had caught Ben in the chest with the force of a giant club; it had stopped his lunge dead in its tracks. The other hoof had caught Big Ben squarely between the eyes. He went down in a crashing fall that sent dust flying.

It was over almost as soon as it had started. Bart eased up his hand grips and seesawed the cotton reins until he had the big horse aimed toward the yard, then applied a little leg pressure. The bay horse responded while looking around at the inert animal on the ground behind him.

Bart wanted in the worst way to dismount and go back to see whether Big Ben was alive or dead. Instead, he forced the bay horse to continue toward the yard, and for a fair distance the big bay horse obeyed, but there was still fire in his blood.

He was within a hundred or so feet of the open corral gate when he wrenched the cotton reins through Bart's fingers and got his head down.

He fought the man on his back as hard as he had fought the Perry brothers. He sunfished and teetered high on his back legs, then hurled himself forward and downward, striking with both front legs as stiff as iron posts. Bart's hat flew off his head, his entire body took the sledgehammer-shock of the landing.

If the big horse had shied, he would have lost his rider—Bart's vision was blurred. But the big horse bucked in a straight line. He bucked hard and bawled; he hit the ground with a thousand pounds of jolting force, and as they were about to enter the corral he finally sashayed to the left, hurling the man off his back to the left.

Bart's upper right arm and shoulder struck the tall gatepost when he fell. The bay horse reached the center of the corral and turned to face Bart, who could see the animal's nostrils wide, eyes bulging, sweat darkening every inch of his hide. In the adjoining corral the three broke colts rammed into one another in a far corner and remained there as Bart pushed against the ground with his left arm until he could sit up.

The bay horse watched him and ducked his head several times, snorting softly.

Bart waited for his vision to clear, then, using the tall post to lean against, got to his feet with his right arm hanging limply at his side. He pushed with his remaining strength until he had the gate closed with himself on the outside, then he fainted.

Dusk was coming when he opened his eyes again; the heat was gone. Sixty feet away inside his corral the bay horse was lipping at hay stalks in the dust with the hackamore reins hanging down one side of his neck and with the saddle still securely in place.

Bart sat up and spat dust. Judging from the shadows on the back of the barn, he guessed he had been lying there most of the afternoon. He tried to stand, but it took three times before he succeeded. When he started for the house, he was as unsteady as a drunk, but he got over there, staggered inside, reached his whiskey jug, and took three straight swallows, then collapsed on a kitchen chair and sat there until darkness forced him to try to light the coal-oil lamp. He could not use his right arm but got the lamp lighted anyway, took another couple of swallows from the jug, and stood up.

His right arm was broken above the elbow and his shoulder did not feel much better, although he could move it. He waited for the whiskey to take effect, then went back outside and leaned on a porch post until he thought he was strong enough to make it to the corrals.

The bay horse was drowsing. He roused only when he heard the gate open. He raised his head toward the injured man but made no move to charge at him or to wheel away from him.

Bart got the saddle and hackamore off using only his left hand and arm. He dragged the saddle out of the corral and left it beyond the gate, then forced himself to carry forkfuls of feed to the big horse, as well as to the three colts in the adjoining corral.

After that he had to sit down and rest. Darkness was closing in before he stood up and began to walk resolutely back northward. The arm and shoulder hurt each time he took a step, but he got back where the fight had taken place and by weak starlight looked for Big Ben.

There was no sign of him or of the mares and colts.

He sat on the churned ground until the pain lessened, then arose and limped back to the yard where he had to rest again, although the house was no more than a hundred and fifty feet away.

Inside, the lamp was still burning. He blew down the mantle bringing full darkness inside the house, and staggered off to his bed.

In the morning he had a splitting headache. His arm was terribly swollen and discolored, while his shoulder ached even when he breathed shallowly.

Sunlight was streaming in a window, but he made no move to leave the bed for a full hour, and then he only went as far as the kitchen water bucket, drank until he felt waterlogged, then went out back to the wash-rack to cleanse his face as best he could with his left hand.

He remained on the side porch waiting for some of the pain to diminish. Some of it did, but the broken arm was painful, even when he was standing perfectly still.

There was a rider in the middle distance with sun at his back. Bart moved around to the front of the house and stood in overhang shade awaiting the arrival of the horseman.

It was Nan Holbrook riding a dappled mare. Bart went to the steps and sat down. She saw him as she entered the yard, rode directly up to the house, and as she dismounted to tie up, she said, "What happened? I saw your remount horse with his mares on the east range. He had blood on his muzzle and a terrible swelling to his head."

Bart watched everything she did without making a sound until she came up beside him on the porch steps. She stared at him. He was filthy, unshaven, his shirt was torn, and she could see purple swelling through torn cloth. As she sat down, she said, "Bart, how did you get hurt?" and before he could reply she also said, "There is a doctor over at our place. That's what I rode over to talk to you about. He examined my father and said he thought he could remove the arrowhead without crippling him. I needed someone to talk to. My father is afraid of the operation. You know how I feel. I wanted to talk to you about it." She stopped speaking, sat a moment regarding Bart, then said, "I'm sorry. This can't be important to you right now. Tell me what happened."

He told her, beginning with his ride out of the yard on the bay horse and finishing with his falling into bed last night barely able to move.

She swung to look in the direction of the corrals where the three colts and the big bay horse were all standing against the stringers looking in the direction of the house. They were patiently waiting to be fed. She turned back as she said, "I'll go get the doctor and bring him back. Are you sure the arm is broken?"

He was sure. As she raised a hand to touch it he winced. "It's broken," he said. "I can feel the bones grate. I think I broke it when he threw me against the gatepost. But I can ride, Nan. It would save a lot of time if you'd saddle a horse for me so's I could ride back with you to see the doctor."

She stared at him. "You can't ride, Bart. You look terrible. If you fainted and fell off . . ." She jumped up. "I'll help you back to bed and you stay there until I come back with Dr. Mailer." She leaned toward him to help him rise but he got to his feet unassisted. He let her guide him inside to his bedroom, though. As she was turning toward the door, he said, "Do me a favor before you go, Nan. Feed the horses?"

She stopped and turned in the doorway, smiling at him. "Yes . . . Bart, has it ever occurred to you that, living alone so far from town and from your neighbors, you could get killed on a green horse someday and no one would know about it maybe for weeks?"

Then she was gone and he sank back on the bed and closed his eyes.

CHAPTER 5

The Unexpected Meeting

He had no idea how long he had slept until voices awakened him. Nan had returned with someone and they were in the parlor. Shadows across the bedroom were high on the wall where they always were in midafternoon. He had slept at least four hours.

He called and Nan came down the dingy hallway and stopped in the door opening. Behind her was a burly older man with graying hair. Bart was unable to see him very well until Nan moved toward the bed from the doorway and the burly man stood framed in the opening. He recognized Bart at the same moment Bart recognized him. Neither of them spoke but Nan stopped beside the bed and after looking critically at Bart, forced a smile and gestured toward the muscular older man as she introduced him. "This is Dr. Frank Mailer, Bart. Dr. Mailer, this is the man I told you about, Bart Templeton." She leaned to part torn cloth and disclose the badly swollen arm and shoulder. The burly man's eyes swept from Bart's face to the discolored flesh. He stepped closer and probed with surprisingly gentle hands. After his examination he spoke without looking into Bart's face.

"Broken between the shoulder and elbow. As swollen as it is, we'll have trouble setting it."

Nan asked about the shoulder and the burly man straightened slightly before replying. "Badly bruised. Nothing is broken, though. It will recover before the arm does. Nan, I'll need something to make splints out of, and if you'll fetch my saddlebags, we can get to work."

After she left the room the burly man's gaze rose to the face of the man on the bed.

Bart said, "Mr. Jones . . ."

The burly man's wide-lipped mouth pulled sardonically upward at the corners. His gray eyes showed something they had not shown at their previous meeting, a hint of hard humor. "Have you been back to the wagon-camp since you left, Mr. Templeton?"

Bart hadn't and turned his head from side to side. "Meant to, but just never made it. As soon as I can ride, I'll go back up there." He continued to eye the older man. "Dr. Mailer . . . ?"

The man Bart had known as Tom Jones pulled up a chair and sat beside the bed. "That's right."

Bart thought a moment, then said, "It's a long, hard ride through the mountains from Stillwater, isn't it?"

The burly man gazed a long time at his patient before speaking again. "Six days, Mr. Templeton. You're pretty good at guessing."

"Maybe. Six days getting this far, and three days with those emigrants. Mr. Jones, you could have been halfway to Mexico."

The burly man leaned back in the chair without taking his eyes off Bart Templeton. "I suspect you're right. Tell me, Mr. Templeton, if you came onto a hemorrhaging woman who had just gone through a bad birthing, and knew how to stop the bleeding, would you have ridden on past to Mexico?"

Before Bart could reply, Nan returned with a pair of

saddlebags slung over her shoulder, and several flat pieces of kindling from the woodbox in the kitchen.

Tom Jones went to work with strong hands and an air of impressive confidence. After he dosed Bart with laudanum he told Nan what to do. They pulled until the bones met, and with Nan keeping the pressure on, Tom Jones began splinting and bandaging the arm.

Bart felt nothing. He heard the bone-ends grate together and he watched Tom Jones, but there was no pain. The burly man was methodical, silent, and expressionless as he worked, pretty much as he had been up at the wagon-camp when he and Bart had first met. He was an individual who inspired confidence and when he finally tied the bandaging and straightened up with a nod for Nan to release the broken arm, Bart noticed for the first time that he was not wearing that ivory-handled six-gun.

Bart told Nan where the whiskey jug was and as she went to find it, he nodded in the direction of the chair. As the burly man eased down, Bart said, "You know how to set bones."

The man nodded without meeting Bart's gaze and said, "—And stop bleeding, and keep newborns alive, and do surgery."

"And rob banks?"

That brought the hard gray eyes to Bart's face, but Nan came back with the jug and the burly man hoisted it, swallowed a couple of times, and leaned to place it on the floor beside the bed. When he straightened up and their eyes met again, Bart made a tight little smile. "I sure owe you, Doctor."

The older man continued to hold Bart's gaze as he replied. "You know how to repay me, Mr. Templeton?"

Bart knew and nodded his head. He didn't know what had made a man of Frank Mailer's caliber blow a bank vault and get his companion killed in the escape, then flee with eleven thousand dollars of stolen money, but Mailer's was a safe secret with him.

Nan asked about the shoulder, so Dr. Mailer leaned toward Bart to make an additional examination. As before when he leaned back, he said, "It'll mend in time. I'd hazard a guess, though, that fifteen years from now rheumatism will settle in the joint and you'll suffer." He started to stand up, but Nan said, "As I told you on the ride over, Doctor, the reason I found Bart in his present condition was because I came to talk to him about the operation on my father. . . . While the three of us are together, could we discuss it now?"

The burly man's direct gaze lingered on Nan's face briefly before he answered her. "Yes, I suppose so." He turned toward Bart, cleared his throat, and began speaking, his voice lacking inflection, his face expressionless, his eyes fixed on the far wall.

"It would be a delicate bit of surgery," he continued, "at any time, but as I told Mr. Holbrook and Nan, it probably could have been satisfactorily undertaken a month or two after Mr. Holbrook was shot. The problem now, after so many years, is that the bone has certainly grown around the arrowhead. The doctors he talked to in Denver undoubtedly hesitated to commit themselves because of that, and while I am reasonably sure the arrowpoint can be removed, the damage from removing it now is where the danger lies. Bones do not mend rapidly. Even simple breaks like your arm require a good bit of time to completely heal, and an old wound, such as Mr. Holbrook has, will be a long time healing. His age has a lot to do with it too. But I think I can remove the arrowpoint without crippling him, provided the point of the arrowhead has not penetrated the vertebrae, in which case it may be within a fraction of an inch of his spinal nerves and cords. If he has the operation, the important thing will be to work the point free from in back and extract it very gently, before it can sever nerves and cords."

His gaze went from Nan to Bart, both of whom remained silent. Finally he said, "It's very dangerous, but I think I can do it."

Bart, who had not taken his eyes off the older man's face, said, "Have you ever done anything like this before?"

Mailer's eyes flickered with a glimmer of humor. "No, and I doubt if many other surgeons have. Arrowheads in people's backbones must be one of the rarest injuries on record, Mr. Templeton."

Bart swung his attention to the handsome woman at his bedside. "Nan . . . ?"

"If the chances are fifty-fifty—Bart, it's a living death for him now. If the arrowhead doesn't eventually cripple him, whiskey will do worse. If you were my father, would you take the chance?"

Bart nodded his head. "Yes, but I'm not your father."

Dr. Mailer's expression seemed to soften as he spoke to Nan. "You're lucky he turned to whiskey instead of laudanum. Narcotics addicts almost never break the habit, and it kills. Whiskey may kill, too, but it would take much longer and as a habit, it can be overcome more easily." Mailer slapped his legs and shot up from the chair with the saddlebags in his hand. He held them out. "Would you put these back on the saddle for me, Nan?"

She suspected he had made that request so that he could be alone with Bart, but she took them and left the room. Frank Mailer looked down at his patient. "Don't use that arm for anything, not even shaving. Give it plenty of time. . . . There is one other consideration concerning her father's condition—you."

Bart understood. "Don't worry about it, Doctor."

"Of course I'll worry about it. Even if you never open your mouth, I'll still worry about it."

"No one will ever find out anything from me. Anyway, I just made a guess." As he spoke Bart eyed the burly man askance. "Tell me something: How did you happen to be over at the Holbrook place?"

"I was within sight of their buildings when my horse stepped in a prairie-dog hole and pulled up lame. I led him to their yard to try and buy another animal. It was close to suppertime. The old man and I sat on the porch with some watered whiskey and talked. He told me what has evidently been uppermost in his mind for a long time."

"You told him you were a surgeon?"

Frank Mailer soberly nodded his head. "Yes. So he asked me to stay over and I did. . . . Foolish, wasn't it? For the second time I let someone's misery slow me down."

Bart looked past him in the direction of the doorway. "Do it," he said softly. "I got faith in you, Mr. Jones. So does Nan, or she wouldn't be as worked up as she is. Do it."

Mailer finally smiled. It made his otherwise forbidding features look youthful. He leaned, placed a big hand on Bart's injured shoulder very lightly, and said, "I'll do it if I can convince him it's worth the risk. Because I trust you."

Bart smiled back. "I don't know anything."

The older man went to the doorway before speaking again. "I'll ride over in a few days to look at the arm. We can talk."

After he was gone Bart raised up while the laudanum was still working, hoisted the whiskey jug with his left hand, and took a couple of swallows. As he was lowering the jug, it occurred to him that he had drunk more liquor since yesterday than he normally drank all year.

Nan reappeared in the doorway to say she had fed the horses and would be back the next day. Then she looked at him and also said, "How does he impress you?"

"Like a man who feels for other folks, even if he doesn't look like he does. . . . Can you talk your pa into the surgery?"

She shrugged slightly. "I've been trying and I'll keep on trying."

"Nan . . . thanks. For what you've done, I'm going to give you that chestnut horse with the light mane and tail. I've been riding him. He'll make you the best saddle animal you ever owned."

She colored. "No. You don't owe me anything. I'll see you tomorrow." She hurriedly left the house.

Bart slept, awakened once as nightfall arrived, then went back to sleep.

He awakened at his usual time, about an hour before sunrise. Only his shoulder hurt, and it did not hurt with nearly the intensity of the day before, so he arose and went to the kitchen to light the lamp, heat water, and try shaving with his left hand. It was not a great success, but it was better than having his face itch.

Dawn was brightening when he got down to the barn to pitch feed with one hand. As the sun rose over the range, he leaned on the corral watching the bay horse lip up his hay.

The horse scarcely more than acknowledged his presence by casting an occasional look toward the place where Bart was leaning. He had stopped leaking blood and his rear legs showed no swelling.

As Bart turned away in the direction of the barn, he sighted distant movement to the north. It was the brood mares grazing toward the yard with Big Ben.

Bart went to the house to put the coffeepot on and fry some potatoes and meat for breakfast. After he had finished eating, he went outside and saw that the loose stock was much closer. Evidently his remount stud had learned nothing because he had picked up the scent of the wild horse and was standing like a picture-postcard stallion testing the air and straining to find his adversary.

Bart returned to the corrals as Big Ben began herding the mares away before approaching the round corral where the bay horse was still eating, oblivious of the presence of the loose stock nearby.

When Ben was close enough, Bart walked out toward

him. This time Big Ben allowed the man to interfere with his purpose. He even put his head down as he usually did to get his forehead scratched.

There was swelling and broken skin, but despite the force of the strike that had knocked him senseless, the bone was intact under Bart's exploring left hand.

The blow to his chest had resulted in a deep gash. Bart returned to the barn for ointment and again Big Ben stood like an old gentle horse while he was greased to keep the flies from blowing the cut and to also hasten its healing.

Finally Bart waved his hat and swung his one good arm to make Big Ben go out and join his harem. The horse went, but he stopped halfway between Bart and the mares to cast a malevolent look in the direction of the round corral. The bay horse did not even lift his head from the flake of hay he was eating. As far as he was concerned, what had happened between Big Ben and him was history.

CHAPTER 6

The Horsemen

Nan arrived in her father's top buggy. She had a wicker hamper in back. Bart wrinkled his nose at the aroma as he lifted the hamper for her. "Fried chicken?"

She laughed and replied, "Fried chicken. How do you feel?"

"Much better."

"I'll feed the horses."

"I already fed them," he said and told her about his remount stallion bringing the mares and colts down close to the yard. He mentioned Big Ben's condition and what he had done to alleviate it as best he could. Then he placed the hamper in the shade by the barn, took her driving horse from between the shafts and led it inside to be stalled and fed. She helped, particularly in removing the driving harness. Afterward, when he picked up the hamper and headed for the house, she walked beside him and she said, "My father finally agreed," then waited for Bart's reaction.

He stopped to face her. "I'm glad. When will they do it?"

"In a few days. Dr. Mailer wants it done at the ranch."

Bart scowled. "Why not over in Holtville?"

She shrugged. "He is making arrangements to do it at the ranch. I mentioned town, but he didn't seem to like the idea."

Bart's brow smoothed out. Tom Jones would have a good reason for not wanting to draw the kind of attention to himself old Holbrook's surgery would be certain to arouse in Holtville.

They went into the house and through to the kitchen where he put the hamper atop the old table. He went out back to wash his hand. When he came back she had arranged the food on plates. There were even gingham napkins.

He stood a moment looking at her. He had met her about a year after staking his claim. They had become friends with an easy, half-serious, half-joking kind of relationship. That she was beautiful he had noticed at their first meeting but he had left it at that. She was the daughter of John Holbrook, one of the biggest and wealthiest cattlemen in the territory. He had nothing but a band of brood mares, a remount stallion from the government to upgrade his horses, about a thousand acres—of which only one hundred and sixty was deeded land—and nothing else except his log buildings and about twenty years of experience with cattle and horses, mostly with horses.

He had never had illusions about his ability to make a lot of money, and he was content. Almost any cowboy working for her father was as well off; at least the top-hand and range-boss made as much as he did.

He had never seen her as animated as she was today. When she looked up and saw him watching her, color rose into her face, but she did not lower her eyes. She smiled at him.

"Are you hungry?" she asked.

He laughed. "Always. Did you cook the chicken?"

She pointed to a chair and he sat down. "Yes. You didn't know I could cook, did you?"

He had never thought about it. In fact, he had never thought about her in any way except atop a horse. He looked at the plateful of food in front of him. He looked at his right hand held in a splint across his chest. "I wouldn't dare tell you how I feel right this minute," he said.

She sat opposite him, black hair showing at high shine, dark eyes watching his face with genuine liking. "Tell me anyway," she said.

He continued to regard the meal in front of him. "You won't like it. You'll get mad."

"Bart . . . ?"

"All right. With a meal like this and one hand to eat it with I feel like a one-legged man at a butt-kicking contest."

She blinked, then laughed. "Eat," she commanded, and he obeyed.

For a long while they were silent until he asked when her father would have the surgery and she replied between mouthfuls. "Next Wednesday. This is if Dr. Mailer has everything arranged the way he wants it."

"In the house?"

"Of course in the house. In his bedroom."

"Will he do it alone?"

"He wants me to assist. I don't know anything about surgery."

He paused and raised his head. "Will you faint, Nan?"

"I've never fainted in my life, Bart."

He chewed and swallowed before speaking again. "But this will be something you've never faced before. He'll be working on your father and there will be blood."

She reached for a coffee cup before replying. "He told me what to expect. I can do it."

"Anything I can do?"

She smiled, setting her cup in the saucer. "You can ride over if you'd like, but as far as I know, there's nothing anyone but Dr. Mailer can do."

He nodded. "I'll come over. Maybe afterward you'll need someone to hold your hand."

She looked steadily at him for a moment, then lowered her eyes to the plate as she spoke. "All right. Be there early."

He finished eating, draining his cup of coffee, and sat back regarding her. "Does it worry you?"

She answered honestly. "Yes."

"Me too. He set my arm like a professional, but I've known range-riders who could set bones."

Her black gaze swept back up to his face. "You have doubts about him, Bart?"

"Well, not exactly. But he came out of nowhere leading a lame horse, and next week he's going to do surgery on your father's back, something other doctors wouldn't do." He thought of the emigrant woman. It wasn't exactly true to say Tom Jones had come out of nowhere, but he could not tell her what Tom Jones had done for the emigrant woman.

He went on, "I guess I shouldn't have said that, Nan. I have faith in him. Your pa must have faith in him, too, or he'd never have agreed to this."

"Faith," she replied reflectively, "and desperation. He knows what the drinking is doing to him. And he knows that unless this succeeds, he's going to be in more and more pain as he gets older. We sat in the parlor last night after everyone else had gone to bed and talked about a great many things, and we always came back to what he has decided he has to do." She looked steadily at Bart for a moment before continuing. "He knows his life is not in danger, but he told me that if the surgery fails and he can't use his legs afterward, he would rather die."

Bart reached for his half-empty coffee cup. It was hard to imagine being unable to walk, to ride, to have the use of one's legs. He drained the cup and put it aside. "How did he get that arrowhead in his back?"

"Shortly after I was born he and my mother rode into the

mountains north of Wild Horse Mesa where they had a special place; near a little waterfall in a meadow. They spent three days up there. There were still holdouts in the mountains back then. On the third day as he was saddling the horses for the ride back, an Indian who was hiding among the trees shot him. My mother always said it must have been a young hunter, because grown men did not use those little obsidian bird-arrowpoints. But they never knew. She got him home, and the army made a sweep but found nothing except an abandoned *ranchería* where the Indians had spent the winter. That's all anyone ever knew.''

He continued to gaze at her after she had finished speaking. She was a full-bodied woman with humor and beauty and tough resourcefulness. Someday some man would come along. . . .

She startled him. ''What are you thinking?''

He reddened. ''Just thinking.''

''Can I guess?''

He shrugged.

''You were thinking about my father.''

''I was thinking about you.''

Her breath ran out slowly, but as before she did not flinch from his stare, even though he had stopped her dead in her tracks. Moments later she said, ''Do you feel like walking down to the corrals?''

They went outside. The day was waning; there were red-streaked clouds across the sky. She fed the horses for him, then they leaned together watching them eat. The bay horse accepted Bart but evinced interest in the woman. He chewed and watched her. She noticed that nearly all his injuries had healed and had hair growing over them. Then she said, ''Fifteen dollars for him.''

Bart laughed and pointed to the handsome chestnut gelding in the adjoining corral. ''That's your horse. When I come over next Wednesday, I'll lead him along, then I'll ride back without him.''

She studied the chestnut horse for a long time without speaking. "Bart, he'll bring you up to fifty dollars in Holtville. He's beautiful." She faced him. "I couldn't accept him. I really couldn't."

He said nothing for a while; he sensed that she had some reason other than the fact that the horse was too valuable to be given away that restrained her from accepting the gift. After a long interval of silence he said, "You got a long drive ahead of you, and it'll be dusk directly."

Nothing more was mentioned about the chestnut gelding. She returned with him to the house for the hamper, then helped him back her buggy horse between the shafts and secure the tugs to the single tree. He eyed the harness; it was a California set and lacked hames, a collar, and a collar pad. He had seen them before but had never owned such a harness. What he had hanging in the barn was the heavier variety with a collar and hames. As he handed her up into the buggy, she said, "I enjoyed myself."

He smiled up at her. "I'm grateful, Nan. You're a good cook. Thanks for coming over and looking after me." He wanted to say something more personal, more heartfelt, but could not find the words.

She evened up the lines and smiled at him. "I'll be back. Probably not tomorrow but the day after."

"You don't have to worry about me," he told her. "I'll get along. But if you're over this way . . ."

She turned the rig and headed back the way she had come leaving him standing in the late afternoon gazing after her. After being acquainted with her for three years, today for the first time he'd had distinctly masculine feelings about her.

He wagged his head and strolled out back to look at the big bay horse. The animal was still eating, but he must have been nearing his capacity because he left the hay and walked over to the man and pushed his head out until Bart could reach his forehead. He had never done that before. In fact, he had never before reacted to the man's presence with anything but wariness.

Bart stroked him and talked to him until he abruptly yanked away and whirled, head up, ears forward, staring northward through the setting late-day diminishing daylight.

Bart went as far as the gate before he could see out where the horse was staring. There were four horsemen loping steadily toward the yard. They were very distant. Even if the light had been better, they would have been too far for Bart to make out anything distinctive about them.

But they had come from the north, from the vicinity of Wild Horse Mesa. Maybe from beyond Wild Horse Mesa. His heart almost stopped. From Stillwater up in Wyoming?

Nan had said possemen were searching the countryside for the escaped bank robber. In fact, he remembered her mentioning that manhunters were combing the area between Stillwater and Holtville.

He thought about the element of time. If that bank robbery had occurred something like two weeks earlier and those were indeed manhunters, even granting that they'd had to track their prey through about a hundred miles of mountainous country, they should have reached Blue Basin before this.

His hope that they were not possemen vanished after they reached his yard and he saw the badge on the shirt of their leader. He was a thick, dark man with about a ten-day growth of salt-and-pepper beard. The leader swung to the ground, yanked off a glove, and extended his hand as he said, "I'm Deputy Jess Morris from Stillwater. These gents are possemen. We been trailing a bank robber named Jones. Tom Jones. He dynamited the vault at the Stillwater bank and made off with eleven thousand dollars in greenbacks. Him and a friend. The friend got shot before he could make it out of town, but Jones got clean away and come south. We been on his trail ever since."

Having said all that, Deputy Morris pulled off his other glove, shoved them both under his shellbelt, and stood looking around the yard as his companions led their animals to the barn tie rack.

With enough time to order his thoughts, Bart offered them his hospitality and led the way into the barn where they off-saddled as they talked. Deputy Morris seemed to be an open, forthright individual. He described the bank robbery, including the killing of one of the outlaws, then he accounted for the days when he and his companions should have been down in Blue Basin by saying, "We come onto an emigrant camp in the north foothills. A woman with a new baby and her man; sodbusters from back east heading for Oregon."

Bart leaned on the saddle-pole watching the men and saying nothing.

Deputy Morris brought his saddle over and heaved it upon the pole, then smiled as he straightened up, looking squarely at Bart. "First break we've had. We spent a couple of days at their camp." Morris's bold dark eyes looked coldly at Bart Templeton. "Seems the lady was hemorrhaging after birthing, and this feller came riding down out of the mountains and knew what to do . . . His name is Tom Jones."

Bart murmured something noncommittal; instinctive caution warned him to be silent.

Morris turned to watch his companions, tipped back his hat, and without looking at Bart, he said, "They said a stockman rode up to the camp, told them they was on his land, but it'd be all right to stay until the lady was fit to travel." Slowly Morris's head came around. "His name was Bart Templeton. He told them where his yard was, and we followed the directions they gave us. You'd be Bart Templeton?"

Bart nodded his head, giving the bearish older man look for look. "Yes."

"Well, then," said Deputy Morris, "not long after you left their wagon-camp, so did Tom Jones. And they watched him heading south—but mostly southeast. Mr. Templeton, answer me straight out: Since you met Jones up yonder, have you seen him?"

Bart had suspected the deputy sheriff was leading up to this question, so he was not caught entirely unprepared for it. "He didn't say a whole lot up yonder where we met, Sheriff, and after I got back, I got this busted arm from that big bay horse out back. Not a soul came around for some time. If he came south, he didn't come here. If he went southeast, he most likely didn't even cross my land."

"What's east of you, Mr. Templeton?"

"A big cattle outfit owned by a man named John Holbrook. He keeps four riders year-round, owns more land than a person could ride over in a week. Been in this country a long time. Runs a lot of cattle and some horses. Me, I just run horses."

The deputy was interested. "About this Holbrook fellow, would you say someone with eleven thousand dollars in his saddlebags could buy his protection?"

Bart almost smiled as he shook his head. "Mr. Holbrook is a wealthy man. He owns buildings over in Holtville, uses only expensive purebred bulls on his grade cows. And he's one of those old-time cowmen who wouldn't even mark a slick calf. No, Mr. Morris, as long as I've known the Holbrook outfit and as long as I've been in this part of the country where folks have known them even longer, I've never heard even a whisper of dishonesty connected with his name. If your fugitive crossed Holbrook land heading toward Mexico, he'll be a long way south by now. But one thing's sure as hell, he'd never be able to buy shelter from old John Holbrook."

The deputy's quiet, rough-looking companions walked over after stalling their horses. One of them pouched a cud of chewing tobacco in his cheek. He was also graying, and his face was lined and weathered. He was wizened and not too tall.

Jess Morris glanced at his companions and let out a noisy sigh. "Looks like we can either push on or go back, gents."

The grizzled man with the puffed-out cheek eyed Bart dispassionately. "How about you," he asked. "What would you do for three or four thousand dollars?"

Bart began to redden as he straightened up off the saddlepole, and before he could reply, Deputy Morris looked darkly at the shorter man with the cud of tobacco in his cheek. "Walter, you said it yourself when we quartered for tracks—there wasn't no fresh sign coming down in this direction. Now then, let's not abuse this gent's hospitality. It'll be dark soon, and I'm hungry as a bitch wolf." Morris turned with a smile toward Bart. "Nothin' meant, Mr. Templeton. All four of us been on the trail a long time; it hasn't done no one's disposition much good."

CHAPTER 7

A Matter of Belief

It was a little crowded in the kitchen after Bart set out his whiskey jug, four tin cups, saw his guests settled, and went to work at the cook-stove.

Darkness fell quickly, a wolf howled about the time the moon rose, and there was a hint of chill in the night. But in the log house it was warm and comfortable. As the Stillwater possemen sat hunched around the kitchen table depleting Bart's jug, they talked about the bank robbery.

Only two aspects of the affair really interested Bart, and during a lull in the talk, he asked Deputy Morris about Tom Jones.

The whiskey on an empty stomach had made Jess Morris relaxed and garrulous. "It's an odd story," he said, swinging one thick arm over the back of the chair watching Bart at the stove. "Tom Jones ain't his name. It's Frank Mailer, and the fellow who run the bank at Stillwater is his brother-in-law. Well . . . he *was* Mailer's brother-in-law. Mailer's wife upped and died about seven years ago somewhere back east where Mailer was running a doctoring business. They say he was a good physician and surgeon, but I don't know about that. All we knew around Stillwater was that his brother-in-law, whose name is Heber Henderson, come out west and started up the bank at Stillwater not long after Mailer's wife died. He started it with fifteen thousand dollars of his own money. The bank prospered right from the start. There's a lot of ranches and storekeepers and whatnot in the Stillwater country. They was tickled pink when Mr. Henderson started up his bank.''

Deputy Morris reached for his jug, swallowed twice, and pushed the jug back toward the center of the table before resuming his tale.

"Like I said, that was about seven years ago. Since then, the bank's done real well. Mr. Henderson built a two-storied house, drove a real nice rig to a pair of matched sorrel horses, and married my boss's daughter—the sheriff's daughter. Then, about six months or such a matter ago, a man calling himself Tom Jones showed up at one of the cow outfits and got himself hired on. I guess from what the man said who hired him, he wasn't much with livestock but he worked hard and learnt fast. Only none of us knew any of this until just lately.

"Tom Jones partnered up with a young drifter named Jack Sunday. It most likely wasn't his name, but it's the only one anyone knew him by. It was Jack who got killed out front of the bank after the robbery. Anyway, him and Tom Jones come into town one morning bright and early a couple of weeks back. Jack got a drink at the saloon, then stood out front of the bank with their horses. No one paid much attention. Jack used to come to town on Saturday nights with the other riders from the ranch, so he wasn't a stranger in town.

"Only this morning Tom Jones went into the bank, walked into this ex-brother-in-law's office and, according to Mr. Henderson, it was one hell of a surprise because he hadn't seen Mailer in over seven years. Mailer aimed his six-gun at Mr. Henderson and cocked it. He told Mr. Henderson he wanted ten thousand dollars in cash. Mr.

Henderson told him he was crazy, he wouldn't give it to him, gun or no gun. So Mailer marched Mr. Henderson over to the vault, told the clerks to lie belly-down on the floor, and when Mr. Henderson refused to open the vault, Mailer produced some dynamite and blew the damned thing. He scooped up all the money while everyone was choking on dust and run outside where Jack Sunday flung him his reins and they made a run for it.

"The saloonman next door had his windows broke by the explosion; he grabbed a gun and run outside and got off one good shot. He hit Sunday and killed him, but Mailer got clean away."

Bart brought plates of fried spuds and meat to the table and placed them in front of his guests. He served Jess Morris last and as he did so, he asked a question. "Why ten thousand dollars? Why not just demand everything that was in the safe?"

Deputy Morris was raising his eating utensils when he answered. "My boss asked Mr. Henderson the same question when we got him out of the bank and over to the jailhouse office. The banker was dazed, his clothes was all tore, and a piece of something had hit him in the face, and he was bleeding. He told us that when his sister was still alive back east, her and Mailer put ten thousand dollars in a safe in Mr. Henderson's store back there. Someone robbed the store and stole all that money. He said Mailer told him when Missus Mailer was dying that he was going to get their money back from her brother if it took him the rest of his life to do."

"And," said the grizzled, tobacco-chewing posseman named Walter, "he sure as hell done it—with an extra thousand for interest."

Bart returned to the sideboard for his own plate of food and brought it back to the table with him. As he sat down, he said, "You're right, Deputy, it's an odd story."

Jess Morris ate in silence. They all did, but Bart at least

was not concentrating on his meal as the others were; he was recapitulating in his mind all Jess Morris had told him. When his guests were easing back with most of the pleats out of their bellies, Bart had an observation to make.

"If they hadn't seen each other in seven years, and if Mr. Henderson showed up from nowhere in your town, does it seem likely to you that he was trying to avoid ever meeting his ex-brother-in-law?"

The dark-eyed deputy pushed his plate away and pulled the coffee cup in close as he replied to that. "Mr. Templeton, I serve the law. That's all I do. I been at my trade over fifteen years. In that length of time I learned never to take sides nor to sit in judgment. All I know is that Tom Jones dynamited the bank's safe and made off with eleven thousand dollars, and like my boss said, it don't matter to us whether ten thousand of that money really did belong to Tom Jones—that's between him and Mr. Henderson, and maybe a judge in a civil law court—what matters to us is that someone dynamited the bank safe, and rode off with all the money he took out of it. And that's bank robbery pure and simple. You understand, Mr. Templeton?"

Bart went after the coffeepot and put it in the middle of the table. He understood. As he watched them deplete the contents of the coffeepot, he got the discussion back to the emigrants up north at their wagon-camp, and this time it was the weathered, sun-bronzed man named Walter who spoke up.

"When we told them who their savior was and what he did up in Stillwater, they wouldn't believe it. Maybe in a way a man can't blame them for that, can he? Mailer saved the woman's life and knew what to do to keep the baby going until she could nurse it. . . . That's where he shaved off his beard too. When Jess showed them the wanted dodger, they told us he didn't look like that no more, that he'd borrowed the emigrant's razor and shaved himself clean."

Two of the men lighted cigarettes. Walter got a cud into his cheek, and Deputy Morris, who, like Bart Templeton, did not use tobacco, refilled his cup and sipped black coffee.

He eyed Bart amiably. "We sure appreciate your hospitality. I got to tell you when we came out of them mountains and didn't see nothing but open country, I figured we were going to have to tighten our belts for one day and maybe for two days. Then we came onto the wagon-camp and from there we found your place. Mr. Templeton, I'm authorized to pay."

When Jess Morris spoke that last sentence he was eyeing Bart closely. A common reaction when that offer was made in cow country was someone's quick and indignant anger. This time the offer was answered with a smile and a negative nod.

The posseman had been in the saddle since sunup, and now they were comfortable in a warm kitchen with full stomachs. The inevitable result was drowsiness. Bart went down to the barn to see them get settled in their bedrolls, then ambled out back to lean on the corral of the bay horse.

His dilemma was clear-cut. So far he had not lied to the Stillwater deputy. He had evaded several direct answers seemingly without arousing suspicion, but if the possemen lingered in the morning, evasion might not be possible.

The way he saw it he could either encourage them to head on southward, or sneak away after they were asleep, ride to the Holbrook place, and warn Frank Mailer. Neither course was foolproof. Jess Morris knew Mailer's trail had gone southeastward from the emigrants' camp, so Morris would undoubtedly head over in that direction when he left the yard tomorrow. In fact, most likely he would ride directly to the Holbrooks' yard.

If Bart sneaked his saddle out of the barn tonight and rode over there, he would be about an hour reaching the Holbrooks' yard, and another hour returning. If any one of the four men in his barn awakened during his absence and noticed his saddle was gone, when he rode back he would probably be riding right down someone's gun barrel.

The bay horse was drowsing, only occasionally cocking a sleepy eye in the direction of his owner. The colts in the adjoining corral were not even that interested, but a shadow emerging from the rear of the barn was interested and because the shadow did not make a sound as it approached the corral, Bart had no idea he was not alone until the deputy sheriff spoke.

"Y'know," Morris said, standing beside Bart as he came up also to lean on the corral, "Walt didn't mean anything when he asked what you'd do for a sizable wad of that bank money." Morris turned slowly to face his host. "Mr. Templeton, I been in my line of work for a long time. You name the situation and I'll give you ten-to-one odds I been in it, including standing beside fellows who are struggling to make an honest living on these little log-house home-steads who see an opportunity to make bean-money through the winter by helping out a fugitive."

Bart stared steadily at the heavier and older man. "You're not standing beside one now," he said evenly.

Morris was silent for a long time, studying his host. Eventually he turned back to looking at the bay horse. "Something else, Mr. Templeton . . . in my line of work you talk to a hell of a lot of folks, and after maybe five or ten years of it you get so's you can feel it when they're telling you the truth and when they ain't."

"I haven't lied to you, Mr. Morris."

The older man barely inclined his head. "I believe you. I also got the feeling this evening that you didn't tell all you knew."

Bart leaned on the corral stringers again and also looked in at his big, newly broke bay horse. "You ever been wrong, Deputy?" he asked.

The lawman turned, openly smiling. "Yeah, plenty of times. I hope I'm wrong this time." He pushed up off the corral and nodded as he padded back toward the barn in his stocking feet, leaving Bart gazing after him, convinced that neither of his courses of action was now possible, certainly not sneaking his outfit from the barn and riding over to the Holbrook place.

But after he was bedded down he could not sleep. Tomorrow was almost certainly going to bring a crisis.

And there was something about Jess Morris. . . . Bart could not define it, but he sensed it.

CHAPTER 8

The Crisis

Bart made a mound of fried meat and piled it atop a platter before his guests trooped up from the barn to enjoy this final installment of his hospitality. When they came in, they were amiable, even the deputy sheriff—although as the others ranged around the table and filled coffee cups, Jess Morris eyed their host more often than any of his companions did. Bart felt rather than saw Morris's attentive glances.

During breakfast Bart could hear his colts nickering to be fed. The grizzled man named Walter was the first to finish eating. He ambled out to the front porch for his morning cud and encountered something that brought him back indoors where he announced that a horseman was coming from the east.

Bart's heart sank; Dr. Mailer had promised to return a few days after setting his broken arm. But it wasn't Frank Mailer, it was Nan Holbrook. She stopped down at the barn to loop her reins at the tie rack and saw four strangers push out onto the porch of the main house to stare at her. One of them was an unshaven older man with a dark look about him who was wearing a badge on his shirtfront.

She finished tying the horse and stood down there until

Bart came out, shouldered past his guests, and started down
to greet her. Behind him, the four possemen followed
along.

Her look of inquiry caused Bart to make a curt explanation. "Posse-riders from Stillwater looking for that man
who robbed the bank up there a while back. This here is
Deputy Sheriff Jess Morris. Deputy, this here is Nan
Holbrook from that big outfit I told you about east of here."

Nan almost imperceptibly nodded her head, but Jess
Morris, who evidently was an individual who appreciated
female beauty, swept off his old hat with a grand gesture and
smiled so broadly it seemed his lips would split. His
companions did the same; they, too, could not refrain from
staring. Out of nowhere had come a variety of female
beauty none of them had expected to find and probably had
never seen the equal of even in large towns.

Nan's eyes settled meaningfully on Bart's face, asking a
silent question. He told her all the possemen had told him,
then concluded by saying that the possemen thought the
outlaw had ridden southeasterly from the foothills. But he
still did not mention the emigrants, so Deputy Morris
completed what Bart had said by explaining about them and
what Mailer had done up there at their wagon-camp, and
this time when her eyes left Morris to return to Bart, they
seemed puzzled.

Bart kept his face expressionless. With Morris standing
close, there was nothing he could say. After a few moments
Nan seemed to recover from her surprise and anxiety. She
said, "I told you I'd ride over to see how you were." She
considered his bandaged arm. "Is it all right?"

He shrugged. Since last evening he had been using his
left arm to do all the work. The right arm was not painful,
and he had been careful of it, so he smiled back at her as he
said, "Fine."

She was quick-witted. "I think I saw your mares and the
remount horse heading for our range. They were too far off

for me to go after them, so I thought maybe if you had the time the pair of us could go up and turn them back."

He looked directly at her. His horses were not on the east range; they almost never went over there, not even when the feed was short late in the year, and Nan knew this as well as Bart did.

He said, "All right. Just as soon as these gents leave I'll get the chestnut horse and we'll go after them." He turned toward the deputy. "Mr. Morris, there is a town named Holtville about sixty miles southeast of here. Maybe the lawmen over there can lend you a hand in looking for your bank robber."

Jess Morris brought his attention back to Bart with an effort. "Maybe," he agreed. "Well, we're right obliged for your hospitality, Mr. Templeton, and don't let us hold you up. We can saddle up at the same time; you go your way and we'll go ours."

Nan accompanied Bart to the rear corrals, where he caught the flashy chestnut horse and led it outside to be tied to the corral before he went after his saddle in the barn. She said, "What do they know?"

"Nothing, as far as I can figure out. I certainly didn't tell them anything."

"Why didn't you ride over and warn us, Bart?"

He heard the anxiety in her voice and saw it in her expression. "I wanted to last night, but the deputy was keeping an eye on me . . . Nan, you'd better ride for it as soon as they leave the yard."

She stared at him with a glassy look. "Dr. Mailer's on his way over here, Bart. In fact, I offered to ride with him, but he had some things to do at the ranch, so I left first. He's out there now on his way over to look at your arm. If they go toward our yard, they're going to meet him. Do they know him by sight?"

"Yes, although when he was in Stillwater country, he wore a beard, but Morris is no one's fool." As Bart finished speaking, the possemen were leading their saddled animals out front. Only one of them, Jess Morris, brought his horse out the back way to seek Bart and offer a hand as he thanked him again for his help and hospitality. Then the deputy stared at Nan Holbrook again before turning to mount his horse and ride around to the front of the barn where his men were waiting.

The possemen raised arms in a high salute as they were leaving the yard on a southward course and got far enough past the barn to see Bart and Nan out beside the corrals. Bart waved back, then went hastily to the barn for his saddle and bridle and blanket.

While he was saddling the chestnut gelding, Nan hurried around front for her horse and returned astride it. She leaned and spoke breathlessly. "You ride due east until you find him. I'm going after the deputy to show him the way to Holtville." She straightened up, looking beautiful in the clear golden sunlight. "I think he'll listen to me," and before Bart could protest, she turned and urged her mount over into a gallop in the wake of the possemen.

He watched for a moment or two, then swore, finished rigging out the chestnut horse, and mounted without bothering to turn the horse a couple of times before getting astride. With this particular horse, it was a safe thing to do. He was green, but he was tractable by nature. Nevertheless, when Bart crossed the yard eastward he did not lift the chestnut gelding out of a walk. He held him at this gait for a quarter of a mile before pushing him over into an easy lope.

He could make out the distant possemen. Nan had caught up to them and the entire party was riding at a steady walk almost due southward. His mouth pulled down at that. Evidently she had charmed Jess Morris; it was not difficult to believe that she had managed this because in the yard he had been unable to take his eyes off her.

The chestnut horse was limber and comfortable to ride. He covered a lot of ground before Bart saw a rider north of where he was loping. He had rather expected Mailer to be on a direct course, about where Bart himself was riding, therefore the horseman he watched might not be the doctor, although it was difficult to imagine who else it could be. He angled to his left, aiming to intercept the distant horseman within a mile or so.

It was indeed Dr. Mailer. Bart recognized him from a couple of hundred yards away and eased down to a walk until the medical practitioner also recognized Bart, and pulled to a halt.

When they met, Bart offered no greeting and did not allow Frank Mailer time to speak. He launched into an explanation of the things that had happened since late yesterday afternoon. When Mailer stiffened in the saddle, peering in the direction of Bart's yard, Templeton told him about Nan's ruse and Mailer loosened a little, gazed at Bart for a moment, then wagged his head as he said, "You were right; if I'd had any sense, I never would have stopped and they never would have overtaken me."

Bart threw a glance to his left, but the possemen and Nan Holbrook were no more than ants moving across the tawny grassland. He faced the older man and said, "I don't know what to tell you. We could go down to my place and I could hide you. I doubt that they'll come back, but I don't think that's much of an answer. Suppose we turn back to the Holbrook place and explain everything to John Holbrook?"

Mailer sat looking gloomily past his horse's ears. "I think that Stillwater deputy eventually will ride into the Holbrook yard. You said you didn't think he was anyone's fool. I can tell you for a fact that he's not. I heard a lot of stories about him up north. I never met him because I made a point of staying out of Stillwater until I was ready to face down my former brother-in-law. Mr. Templeton, that man won't leave Blue Basin until he picks up my tracks going out of here. He has a reputation for being a dogged tracker. Nan may take him partway to Holtville but I'll give you odds she won't fool him. The minute she turns back he will too."

Bart let go a long, loud breath. "John Holbrook. We're not going to be able to keep them away from you without him."

Frank Mailer's mouth pulled down. "I've spent several evenings with Mr. Holbrook, talking about many things. He's given me a number of examples about how he has treated fugitives in the past years. My impression is that he wouldn't help a bank robber if his life depended upon it."

"It damned well may depend on it," stated Bart, raising his left hand with the reins in it. "Your choices are pretty simple. Let me hide you and pray Morris doesn't come back to my place, or we'll both ride over to the Holbrook place and lay it on the line for John. Do you see another way?"

Mailer considered the bronzed features of the younger man. "Only one. I could leave you right now, add horse-stealing to my other crime, ride south to the border, and not look back. Which is what I should have done in the first place, isn't it?"

Bart dismissed the question. "Turn around, Doctor. If John won't help you, then we'll think of something else, but if he doesn't help you—you above just about everyone else because you've given him something to hope for—I'll be as surprised as hell."

The sun was moving past it meridian. It was also changing color as Dr. Mailer stolidly turned back. While they were riding together, he looked over with a faint smile and said, "You seem to be managing fairly well with one arm. Any pain?"

Bart also showed a faint smile. "No pain. Not in the arm, but this other thing is tying my guts in a knot."

"Why?" the older man asked quietly. "It's not your neck they want."

Bart ignored that to ask a question. "Didn't you believe your money was stolen from your brother-in-law's store?"

"I know it wasn't stolen in a robbery, but it was certainly stolen. He stole it."

"Are you sure?"

"Mr. Templeton, the police in Toledo, Ohio, where we all lived at the time, told me emphatically that there was no mark of a forced entry. Whoever broke open Heber Henderson's strongbox at the office in the store did it from inside the building."

"Didn't the police suspect Henderson?"

Dr. Mailer shrugged his shoulders and peered dead ahead. "They did not say whether they suspected him or not. He was on the City Council at the time."

"How did you find him up in Wyoming, Doctor?"

"Waited, Mr. Templeton. Worked and waited. Eventually the Pinkerton people located a Heber Henderson in Stillwater, Wyoming, who operated a bank. There are a lot of Hendersons but not very many Heber Hendersons. I rode the train as far as it went, then rode stagecoaches. Using the name of Tom Jones, I spent two days in Stillwater at the rooming house watching the front of the bank from an upstairs window . . . It was Heber all right. I saw him several times. After that I returned to Toledo and began making plans. Six months later I returned to Stillwater country as Tom Jones, a hired rider." Mailer turned toward Bart. "You know the rest. I'm sure Deputy Morris told you."

Bart nodded. "One more question, Doctor."

"Shoot, Mr. Templeton."

"Who was Jack Sunday?"

Mailer visibly winced before answering. "A drifting range-rider. He was about your age, perhaps younger. Little by little, I told him just enough to get him interested in holding the horses while I robbed the bank."

"Did he knew why you were going to rob the bank?"

"No. He thought I was a professional outlaw, a bank robber. I promised him a lot of money. Someday I'll go back to Stillwater and have a fine big handsome headstone put over his grave . . . Of everything I've done this past year, what happened to Jack is the only thing I regret. And maybe coming down out of those mountains where those emigrants were camped. A quarter mile to the east or west and I would never have seen their camp," Dr. Mailer faced Bart again. "Are you a religious man, Mr. Templeton?"

Bart chose his answer carefully. "I guess in my own way I am. Why?"

"I thought about it as I was working over the emigrant woman. It was not her time to die, and I was the instrument to see that she didn't die."

They could make out the Holbrook rooftops and the large, tree-shaded yard. Two rangemen were loping in from the northeast; otherwise there was no sign of life until they were within a half mile. Two large, shaggy dogs came charging out toward them sounding like wolves and for the first time since Bart had been handling him, the chestnut gelding sucked back as though he might whirl and run, or at the very least, shy violently.

Bart talked to him, stroked his neck, and Dr. Mailer yelled a curse at the dogs. They were either intimidated by his tone of voice or knew him, because they turned back toward the yard without another sound.

The chestnut horse came up in the bit again but kept a wary eye on the pair of dogs as he came around the side of the big log barn into the yard.

CHAPTER 9

Facing Facts

John Holbrook took them to the big parlor of his main house. The room had a large fieldstone fireplace and a considerable amount of heavy leather furniture. On the mantel there were several oil portraits, one of John Holbrook and his wife when they were young. As Holbrook offered them chairs, he eyed them both with a quizzical expression. Neither Bart nor the other older man smiled; Holbrook's intuition told him something was wrong.

It was too early in the day or he would have offered them whiskey and water. As he went to a plain, straight-backed wooden chair and sat down facing them, he said, "Bart, Nan rode over to see you this morning. Didn't you meet her?"

Bart nodded. "Yes, I met her," he told her father, then launched into the whole story.

Holbrook's faded gray eyes widened slightly as Bart talked. Once or twice they wandered to Frank Mailer. When Bart stopped speaking, Holbrook stared steadily at him over an interval of silence, then slowly turned toward Mailer when he spoke.

"Frank, were those possemen looking for you?"

Mailer nodded in silence.

Holbrook hung fire again, but for a shorter length of time, then asked another question of Frank Mailer. "About that bank robbery? Did you do it?"

"Yes."

Holbrook shifted position in his chair, shot a look out the front window, which offered a wide view of the yard, as far as the barn and farther. Then he faced Mailer again. "I'd like to hear about it," he said quietly, and Frank Mailer started speaking in a deep, measured voice. He was still speaking when Bart saw Nan ride into the yard and pass through tree shade toward the barn. He wanted to jump up and go down to meet her. Instead, he sat where he was and listened to the unemotional recital. When Mailer finished, Bart gazed across at John Holbrook to see what effect Mailer's story had had. But John was sitting impassively gazing at the medical practitioner, elbows on the armrests of his chair, large, work-scarred hands lightly clasped in front of his body.

Finally, after a silence that seemed to have been drawn out almost to the breaking point, Holbrook arose and went out to the kitchen. During his absence Mailer and Bart exchanged a look; Bart shrugged his shoulders to indicate that he had no idea what Holbrook's reaction had been.

Burly Frank Mailer sighed and leaned forward in his chair, studying the floor.

Holbrook returned with two cups of black coffee and handed them to his guests, then returned to the kitchen for a third cup. When Holbrook returned and passed Bart on his way to the straight-backed wooden chair, Bart picked up the aromatic scent of Irish coffee—java laced with whiskey.

Someone noisily entered the house from out back. Bart guessed it was Nan. Holbrook and Mailer looked stonily at each other for a moment before Mailer broke the silence.

"It's all right, John. My horse should be over his

lameness by now. I'll go fetch him and be on my way. I didn't want to put you in this position."

Holbrook took a sip and put his cup aside as he spoke. "You are a damned fool, Frank."

Mailer nodded his head in agreement.

"Not about the bank, Frank, about stopping along the way to help folks."

Mailer nodded his head about that, too, and sipped his coffee.

"This is Monday. You were to do my surgery by day after tomorrow.'

Mailer drained his cup before replying. "Go to Denver, John. If they won't do it up there, go back east. There are surgeons who'll do it for you. Keep asking until you find one."

Holbrook made a grimace. "I know I could find one. Your profession isn't much different from mine, Frank; both have risk-takers in them. But I won't take risks with my back . . . Let's get back to these Wyoming possemen." He swung his attention to Bart. "Where are they, and are they likely to come over here?"

From a hall doorway a direct, strong voice answered him as Nan walked into the parlor from the back of the house. "I left them pointing toward Holtville about eight miles southeast of the yard." She went to a leather sofa and sat down, looking directly at her father before continuing. "Mr. Morris is a shrewd man. Behind his smile, he is tough and cunning."

Holbrook said, "Will he go all the way to town?"

Nan shifted a little on the sofa before answering. "That is a two-day ride. I don't think so. He is a tracker and he lost Dr. Mailer's tracks before he reached Bart's place. My guess is that he will circle around and go north until he finds the tracks again."

Her father almost imperceptibly nodded his head. "The damned rain was two weeks early," he muttered. "If he's a tracker, he'll find where the doctor's horse went lame and follow the sign right down to our yard. Two weeks ago the rain would have destroyed his tracks."

Nan was silent. So were Bart and Frank, but Bart's thoughtful gaze was fixed on Holbrook. When he had asked whether his daughter thought Morris would return the implication had been clear to Bart that John Holbrook did not want the Wyoming lawman to find Frank Mailer. That meant Holbrook was thinking in terms of helping Mailer elude capture.

Holbrook raised his eyes to Bart and Frank Mailer. "I guess the question is: When will he show up in our yard? If he shows up tomorrow or Wednesday . . ." Holbrook's wide mouth flattened a little; he stared at his clasped hands. "If he goes as far as Holtville, then returns, we'll have three or four days of grace."

Nan spoke quietly to her father. "He won't go to Holtville."

Her father had evidently come to the same conclusion, because he nodded in agreement with his daughter. After a moment he looked at Bart and said, "I'm fighting for time. This man couldn't have showed up in Blue Basin at a worse possible time for me. I'm staking my life on Frank's ability to make me whole again. After all these years . . . And now this damned manhunter shows up."

Bart drained his cup and leaned to place it on a small marble-topped table beside his chair. As he settled back, he said, "John Morris isn't a cold-blooded individual. If he knew what Dr. Mailer was going to do for you, he'd wait, even if he was right here in your yard. I'll bet a good horse on that."

Holbrook's pale eyes showed temper. "Wait? Wait? Do you think for one minute that if Frank stops my pain I'm going to hand him over to some Wyoming deputy sheriff? You ought to know me better than that by now, Bart."

The silence settled again, and drew out until Mailer broke

it. "Would Morris have jurisdiction outside of Wyoming? What I'm getting at, John, is that I still have the eleven thousand dollars. If he doesn't have authority to arrest me and take me back to Wyoming, maybe if I gave him back the money, he'd settle for that—take it and go back where he came from."

Again the silence settled throughout the large, shadowy room. Eventually Nan spoke. "Pa, suppose you sent one of our riders to Holtville for the marshal."

Holbrook raised a puzzled face. "What good would that do?"

"Stop Deputy Morris from taking Dr. Mailer back to Wyoming by force."

Her father snorted. "We don't need the town marshal from Holtville for that, Nan; we have four riders and our weapons. And we have Bart and me. That'd be enough guns to discourage most deputy sheriffs."

Nan did not yield. "Guns would just make things worse," she said. "Send for the marshal. He has the authority to stop the Wyoming deputy from using force to apprehend Dr. Mailer."

Her father threw up his hands. "All right. But unless he can sprout wings, the Holtville lawman won't get out here in time."

Nan arose and without another word left the room. The men heard her cross the front veranda and go down into the yard in the direction of the bunkhouse. Bart leaned, hoping he'd be able to see her, but she was nowhere near the window. But as he straightened back in his chair he noticed one thing: This day was fast drawing to a close.

Frank Mailer had been studying his host. Now he said, "John, my being here is forcing you to do something you normally wouldn't do—go against the law. When it's dark, I can saddle up and be on my way."

Holbrook was sitting very erect in his wooden chair. He stared at Mailer. "You're right, up to a point," he retorted.

"Answer a question for me, Frank. What you said about your former brother-in-law stealing money from you and your wife, is that absolutely true the way you told it?"

"It is. Absolutely true. She worked as hard as I did to save that much money—his own sister."

Holbrook's gaze roamed the room briefly before settling again upon the other older man. "The way you went about getting your money back was wrong, but the rest of it, I can understand. As for that deputy, you're right. Unless he has extradition papers signed by the governor of Colorado, he's not going to take you anywhere."

Nan returned to announce that she had sent one of the range-riders for the Holtville town marshal. Then she smiled for the first time since entering the parlor and said, "I'll start supper." She looked at the men. "Can I bring you more coffee?"

They declined, and she crossed the room to disappear beyond a wide oak door.

John Holbrook did what Bart Templeton felt like doing, he pulled down a big breath and expelled it in a noisy sigh. He arose from the wooden chair, stepped to the window, and with both hands clasped behind his back, he stood watching dusk settle.

Behind him, Mailer looked at Bart, who smiled. Despite Mailer's dire misgivings, John Holbrook had made his judgment and had come down on the side of Frank Mailer. Undoubtedly his decision had been heavily influenced by personal interest; now that he had made up his mind to submit to surgery on his back he did not intend to let some wandering lawman from out of state make that impossible.

But the decision had more to it than that. Holbrook had been for law and order all his life, but he had never been blind to the inequities of the law, either. Because he believed what he had been told by Dr. Mailer, he stood at the window considering the ways that were available to him to stop the Stillwater deputy in his tracks.

His daughter opposed the use of guns, but John Holbrook had used guns to protect his holdings and his life for fifty years. Even though he understood perfectly well that Judge Colt and his six jurymen could no longer override book-law, Holbrook still thought in terms of violent resistance when there was a need to resist.

Living sixty miles from the nearest town, and having been the law unto himself on the range for so many years, he was not likely to be cowed by the appearance in his yard of someone wearing a badge.

He turned to face his guests and said, "Tomorrow I'll put the riders out to watch. If that deputy shows up with his possemen, he'd better be one hell of a good talker—and even then, he's not going to come in here with demands." He paused, eyeing Bart Templeton. "You'd better spend the night. By the time you'd get back home after supper it'd be close to midnight."

Bart arose from the chair and stretched. He had been sitting for a long time, something he was not accustomed to doing. "I'll go home," he told Holbrook. "I got chores to do, horses to feed. But I'll ride back over tomorrow morning."

"At least stay for dinner."

Nan summoned them to the table in the kitchen. Her face was shiny from standing at the cook-stove, and she smiled when Bart came through the doorway. Her father and Frank Mailer were seating themselves when a heavy set of fisted knuckles rattled the front door. All three men looked up quickly, but it was Nan who went through to the door.

She returned looking mildly surprised to announce that the man who had been feeding the horses down at the barn had heard a wagon and went out to the north end of the yard to make sure. He had told her an old emigrant wagon with two people on the seat was about a half mile away coming directly toward the yard.

Frank and Bart exchanged a look. Bart said, "Those folks from the foothills."

Frank Mailer nodded and arose. "Maybe there's something wrong with the baby. I'll go see."

After he had left the room John Holbrook scowled a little, then his brow cleared as he raised his eyes to his daughter. "More darned company the last few days than we've had all year."

She was drying her hands on a towel and nodded absently at his remark, looking in the direction of the front doorway. Without a word she put the towel aside, brushed back her hair with one hand, then strode across the kitchen and disappeared out into the night in the wake of Frank Mailer.

Her father scowled at his heaping plate, looked at Bart, and said, "Hell," then he, too, arose to leave and Bart followed him.

From the porch of the main house they could see the old wagon behind its pair of big harness horses. Someone was holding up a lantern for the emigrants to see by as they climbed down. All the Holbrook riders were out there, along with Nan and Frank Mailer.

With an inhospitable grunt John Holbrook went down the porch steps with Bart beside him to join the others in front of the barn.

CHAPTER 10

A Surprise

Mailer had guessed right. The emigrant couple had come to the ranch hoping to find help. They were surprised and relieved to see the man they'd known as Tom Jones. The emigrant man had Mailer by the arm by the time Holbrook and Bart Templeton got down there. He was pushing Mailer toward his wife, a sturdy, fair-haired woman who looked pale and drawn, even by lanternlight.

The woman held out her bundled baby to him. "He is sick, Mr. Jones. Can't keep any milk down."

Mailer took the tiny bundle, turning toward the lantern as he did so. Nobody spoke until he glanced back to the baby's parents and said, "Let's take him inside where it's warmer. I think I know what his problem is."

Bart brushed John Holbrook's arm as everyone was turning away from the wagon. "I'll head out now," he said. Holbrook nodded.

Bart went after the chestnut horse and was riding away from the rear of the barn when he looked back. The rangemen were over near their bunkhouse, but Nan, her father, Frank Mailer and the emigrants were nearing the porch of the main house.

It was a pleasant night. It was too early for it to be chilly, and although the moon was little more than a curve of weak orange light, there were stars by the thousands.

Bart let the chestnut horse warm out before boosting him over into an easy lope and holding him to that gait for more than a mile.

His mind was occupied with the events of this day all the way back home. He entered his yard in darkness. A horse heard him and nickered from behind the barn, and as soon as he cared for the chestnut gelding and had flung his saddle over the pole in the barn, he started his one-handed feed routine, beginning with the big bay gelding in the round corral.

It took time to fork in feed to four horses using just one arm. When he was finished, he leaned on the corral for a moment of rest. The horses had been hungry. Now that they had been fed, they paid absolutely no attention to him.

The area was darkly shadowed, and except for the noise of horses eating, it was quiet. He returned to the barn to hang up the pitchfork, then crossed through darkness to the front of the house.

There was a man sitting loosely in a chair on the porch holding a six-gun in his lap. About the time Bart started up the pair of long wooden steps to the porch, the man with the gun got up out of the chair and Bart saw him for the first time. Bart's breathing stopped for two seconds. The man was vaguely familiar, even in the darkness of the porch overhang, as he raised the six-gun to point it.

" 'Evening, Mr. Templeton. I was about to give you up."

The shadowy figure stepped to the edge of the porch to expectorate, and Bart finally knew who he was. The posseman called Walter.

Bart took the final step to the porch, and Walter turned on him with the gun aimed midway between Bart's head and his belt buckle.

"I been askin' myself," said the posseman, "where a

man'd ride to that would take him until darn near midnight to get back.''

Bart leaned on a porch upright without making a sound.

Walter smiled, but he lacked humor as he said, ''Maybe, if I was hiding someone, it'd be some distance from my yard.'' Walter cocked his six-gun, and the smile vanished. ''Where is he? Where you got him hid?''

Bart stared. ''Who?''

''Frank Mailer—Tom Jones—whatever you want to call him.''

Bart shook his head. ''I don't have him hidden anywhere.'' He twisted to look around. ''Where is Mr. Morris and the rest of your crew?''

Walter shifted his cud before speaking again. ''If you don't have him hid, where you been all afternoon and up until the middle of the night?''

Bart answered truthfully but without elaborating. ''I've been over at the neighbors'.''

Walter faintly nodded. ''I wondered about that too. That's a mighty fine-looking woman. Pretty as a speckled bird. . . . Till midnight, Mr. Templeton?''

Bart straightened up off the post. ''Was this Morris's idea, having you come back here and watch the place?''

''Yeah. His idea and mine.''

''Where is he, Walt?''

''North, so's in the morning they can cut Mailer's sign and track him.''

Bart was briefly silent, then moved toward the door. ''You want to go in first and light a lamp?''

Walt turned. ''Naw, you go in first and light the lamp. Tell me something: Why don't you wear a gun?''

Bart was reaching for the latch when he replied. ''Because I'm right-handed, and I broke my arm. I can't even shoot straight with my left hand.''

He went inside, fumbled with the table lamp, got it lighted, and looked back. Walter was standing in the doorway with his cocked Colt. He stepped inside when there was light to see by. He let the hammer down on his weapon and shoved the gun back into his hip holster as he said, "Let's go into the kitchen. My belly thinks my throat's been cut."

Bart led the way, taking the lamp with him. He put it on the table. The posseman pulled out a chair, turned it backward, and straddled it, looking steadily up at Bart. Walt said, "Go ahead and rassle us up a meal." As Bart turned toward the stove to shove dry kindling into the firebox, Walt also said, "I think you been lying to me, Mr. Templeton."

Bart was working at the stove when he spoke. "Walt, Deputy Morris knows that Mailer's tracks didn't come down to my yard."

The weathered, short man watched everything Bart did. "Yeah. But you rode out yesterday. You could have met him somewhere. Mr. Templeton, Jess thinks you know something you didn't want to talk about. So do I." Walt straightened up off the back of the chair as Bart went to a floor-to-ceiling cupboard that was his kitchen cooler. "There is a bounty out. Jess is agreeable to seeing that you get a piece of it."

Bart returned to the stove with two jars, one of meat, the other jar of vegetables. He ignored his armed guest as he put two pans on the stove.

Walt shifted his cud of tobacco again, then lifted his old hat to vigorously scratch for a moment before replacing it. "Could you use a little extra money, Mr. Templeton?"

Bart looked around at the older and smaller man. "Almost everyone I know could use a little extra money."

"Where you got him hid?"

"I told you, I don't have him hid anywhere. I hope you like canned parsnips, Walt."

The posseman watched Bart empty the vegetables into a

pan and put half a dipperful of water in with them. "I don't," he said. "Is that all you got?"

"No. I got a bottle of sauerkraut a lady put up for me last year."

Walt looked pained. "Parsnips'll be all right," he mumbled, and got the subject back where he wanted it. "Jess'll pick up Mailer's sign after sunup. You could save everyone some trouble by telling me what you know about Frank Mailer's whereabouts."

Bart got the second pan filled and heating before he said, "I can't tell you anything. But maybe you can tell me something: Does Deputy Morris think he can ride into Colorado, grab someone, and ride back up into Wyoming with him?"

"Sure he can, if he finds him."

Bart continued to eye the smaller and older man. "Does he have extradition papers signed by the governor of Colorado?"

Walt's expression changed a little, his gaze hardened. "Are you one of them fee-lawyers?"

Bart shook his head. Until this evening he'd had no idea that anyone would need special authorization to take a fugitive back to another state. "Nope, I'm not a fee-lawyer, but I didn't come down in the last rain, either. Does Morris have such a paper, Walt?"

The posseman sat stiffly regarding his host. "Why'n hell don't you just cooperate?" he asked, almost plaintively. "Watch them darned parsnips, they're fixing to boil."

Bart turned back toward the stove, reached high with his left hand to turn down the stove damper, then leaned to stir the cooking meat. "Walt, it's the gospel truth—I don't have Frank Mailer hid out anywhere."

The posseman sighed and leaned with both arms crossed over the top of the chair back. "All right. But you met him. You talked to him. Which way did he go? It'll save us a lot of time if we chase him in the right direction."

"Toward Mexico, for all I know," stated Bart, as he returned to the cupboard for two plates and two cups. He had not put the coffeepot on a burner and only realized it when he removed the parsnip pan. As he set the coffeepot on the burner, he said, "Morris doesn't have an extradition paper, does he?"

Walt arose to step to the back door so he could jettison his cud, then he closed the door and eyed Bart with a hint of defiant hostility. "I've rode with my share of posses," he said, watching his host divide the contents of both pans upon their two plates, "and not more'n a couple of times has anyone needed extradition papers. If you go into a town in another state, why, then, sure, you better have something legal. But mostly where I've rode with posses, it's been even farther from a town than your place is."

Walt went wide around Bart to the opposite end of the table and sat down to pick up his eating utensils. He was, for a fact, very hungry, and as Bart eased down across from him, Walt said, "After we get our man we can be back through the mountains in three, four days, and up to Stillwater in a couple more days. And besides you, who's going to run around saying we snatched Mailer illegally?"

"Mailer can say it," stated Bart, and got a disgusted look from Walt.

"Who is going to believe a bank robber, Mr. Templeton? Once we get him jugged up in Stillwater he can scream until the cows come home, and not a soul will listen to him. And there's something else—if he gets cantankerous on the ride back, he just might never reach Stillwater sitting up atop his horse. He might get there tied belly-down over his saddle. . . . Is that coffee hot yet?"

Bart brought the pot to the table and put it in front of his guest. The coffee was only lukewarm. When Walt tasted it, he grimaced. "How long you been dropping new grounds on top of the old ones in this pot?"

"Two weeks," said Bart wryly.

Walt pushed the offending cup away. "Horse ranching must be starving business to be in if you got to use your coffee grounds over and over."

Bart was not particularly hungry, but since he realized that Walt thought he should be, he ate. After a short pause in their conversation he looked at the older man and asked, "What line of work are you in, Walt?"

Walt's answer came back around an enormous mouthful of food. "Livery business in Stillwater. Livery and horse-trading." Walt chewed like a cow for a while, swallowed, and glowered at his host. "And it pays enough so's I don't have to drink water strained through the same darned coffee grounds for two weeks."

"Where do you figure to meet Morris tomorrow?"

"East somewhere. North and east, up wherever they pick up the tranks." As he said this, Walt rested an eating utensil upright in each hand. "Did Mailer give you some of that bank money?"

Bart almost smiled when he replied. "I'm pushing past thirty-five years, Walt, and in all that time no one has ever given me any money."

"Then, why'n hell don't you just up and cooperate with the law?"

"Which law, Colorado law or Wyoming law?"

Walt lowered his knife and fork as he muttered something under his breath.

Far off, a wolf sounded at the moon. Walt stopped chewing to listen, then continued eating. He looked at Bart and said, "You got mares with colts out there? That damned wolf was pretty close. If he can scent up one of your mares with a baby colt . . ."

Bart nodded. Like all range stockmen, Bart killed wolves on sight because he'd lost several colts to wolves.

Walt finally leaned back, his plate clean. As he fished in a shirt pocket for his plug of tobacco, he said, "You don't mind if I bed down in your barn tonight, do you?"

Bart minded because it was his intention to ride back to the Holbrook place early in the morning. As long as Walt was around, he could not do that. Even if Walt rode off, he might stop somewhere out of sight of the yard and wait to see whether or not Bart rode out—and if so, in which direction.

But Bart said, "No, I don't mind. When you see the deputy, tell him that while he's sashaying around looking for horse sign, Mailer is probably fifty miles away aiming for the Mexican border."

CHAPTER 11

With No Alternative

After Walt went down to the barn Bart cleaned up in the kitchen, then sat with a cup of coffee considering this fresh intrusion into an existence which, for him, had become unusually complicated lately.

He could go down to the barn, catch Walt asleep and tie him up. Then ride out to warn Mailer. The reason he did not do this was he did not want a direct confrontation with Morris and his possemen. They were not positive about any of their suspicions toward Bart, but if he used force against Walt, they would be.

He finished his java and went to bed. It was almost two o'clock in the morning and cold even inside the house.

He ordinarily awakened about four or five in the morning. This time he opened his eyes about five but did not get out of bed for an additional half hour.

He was out back at the wash-rack when Walt came stamping up onto the front porch. Bart had not washed or shaved, but he had doused his hair with water from the stone trough behind the barn and slicked it down.

He was hungry again. So was Walt. The two went into the kitchen. As he was cooking breakfast, Walt sprawled in a chair watching him. Eventually he said, "You going to work around the place today, eh?"

Bart replied without turning from the stove. "This morning, for a while, then I'm going to ride that big bay horse in the round corral."

Both men were silent as Bart served breakfast: fried spuds, leftover cooked meat, and hot coffee, brewed fresh. Walt was halfway finished eating before Bart began. Walt looked up a few times but did not speak until his plate was clean. Then he asked, "How much for the chestnut horse with the light mane and tail?"

"Not for sale," Bart replied.

"Well, how about the big bay horse?"

"Not until I finish him. He's still green."

Walt gave up on horses. "What am I supposed to tell Jess?"

"Whatever you want to tell him, but one thing both of you can damned well believe: I didn't hide Mailer." Bart rose from the table, put his dishes in the big pan of hot water on the stove, then left the kitchen to get his hat. When he returned, Walt had put his dishes in the pan also and was outside on the porch carving a corner off his plug of tobacco. He looked up as Bart came out, then without a word started down off the porch in the direction of the barn.

Bart fed the horses while Walt was rigging out in the barn. When Walt was ready to ride, he led his horse out back and thanked Bart for his hospitality, then he swung up and sat a moment, gazing at the man on the ground before he curtly nodded and reined around on his way northeastward out of the yard.

Bart leaned on the pitchfork, watching as his guest loped across the sunny landscape. After Walt was well out of sight Bart put up the fork, got a shank-rope from the barn, caught the bay horse, and led him into the barn to be saddled. His original intention had been to wait an hour or so after Walt's departure before heading over to the Holbrook place, but the sun was climbing, and he had already wasted enough time.

As he was riding out of the yard he studied the countryside for sign of Deputy Morris's posseman. Walt must have made good time because he was nowhere in view. Still, Bart was wary. He even rode northeastward for a half mile before setting his course for the Holbrook yard.

There were several stands of trees at wide intervals, and although the land looked flat, there were sporadic hills and valleys. In some places the terrain had swales deep enough to conceal a horseman. This was ideal livestock country, with grass as far as a man could see, except to the north where mountainous country marked the boundary of Blue Basin.

Once, more than a mile out, Bart's big bay horse pricked up its ears and turned to gaze northward. But a horse would show interest or curiosity even if all he picked up was the scent of a coyote. As far as Bart could see, there was no movement.

He concentrated on riding, because this horse was not accustomed to being ridden. Since the day of the stud-fight, he had been doing nothing but standing in a corral and eating his head off. But the bay horse walked along as though this were the hundredth sweaty saddle blanket for him instead of only the second or third.

It was a beautiful, golden morning. The kind of day that made a man riding a strong horse feel good all the way down to his toes. Nonetheless, Bart continued to watch the bay horse's ears, and get his "feel" through the seat of his britches. If Bart rode this horse long enough today, the big bay would be broken in if he was ever going to be.

The horse repeated his behavior of an hour or so earlier shortly before Bart had the Holbrook rooftops in sight; he threw up his head and stared off to his left. This time Bart made a closer inspection of the empty land and when that failed to satisfy his curiosity, he turned slightly off-course heading up-country.

For a while he saw nothing except a few birds rising from tall grass at his approach. Then he was passing down the near side of a swale when he saw fresh-shod horse tracks where someone had evidently been riding parallel to him.

He stopped at the bottom of the swale, studied the sign, and instead of climbing out of the swale on the far side, he turned northward and rode along the bottom of the swale until it began rising to meet the higher land. He made the bay horse hump a little to climb out. He halted when he was back atop the prairie to give the horse a breather.

Bart saw the rider about a half mile away. He was headed eastward and appeared furtive, but what probably helped Bart most was that the horseman was watching off to his right, which was in the direction of the Holbrook place. He did not once turn to look back.

Certain who he was riding behind, Bart kneed the bay horse in pursuit. As long as the other rider did not look around, he would not realize he had been flanked, but Bart knew he could not count on this indefinitely, so he began dropping from sight in swales, and riding through bosques of trees. He was north of the rider he was following, and because the bay horse had a thrusting stride, he was closing ground, but instead seemed intent upon watching the ranch a mile south of him.

The rider made an angle to reach a deep arroyo, and Bart watched him descend into it. He squeezed the bay horse over into a jarring trot to get closer before the hidden horseman emerged from the arroyo. But the hidden man did not come out. Bart waited and watched, then decided what his adversary was doing, and squaw-reined still farther northward in the directin of the upper reaches of that arroyo. When he arrived upon the verge and could see down into the arroyo, there was no sign of the other rider. Bart sought a place for the bay horse to slide down and found a narrow, angling deer trail. The bay horse navigated it as though he had been using those narrow trails all his life.

There was sunshine in the arroyo because the sun was almost directly overhead. There was thick underbrush and some trees with tops that barely cleared the sides of the arroyo, making them hardly visible from outside the arroyo. There was a measly trickle of water down toward the arroyo's center, which was also its deepest place. The deer trail ended in grass beside the little creek.

Bart dismounted, left the bay horse tied to a tree, and started southward on foot. He utilized all the protective cover that was available, and there was quite a bit of it.

He saw Walt's horse before he saw the man. The horse either scented Bart's stealthy approach or heard him moving because it was standing like a statue peering in the direction from which Bart was approaching.

The man who had been riding the stocky bay horse was a hundred yards southward crouching upon a ledge just below the topout of the arroyo. He was so engrossed with watching activity in the Holbrook yard he still did not look back.

Bart slipped past the curious bay horse, remaining in dense underbrush until he was almost directly below the crouching man, then he raised up and spoke.

"You won't find your deputy sheriff down there, Walt."

Walt was so startled that, in his haste to twist around, he stumbled. He flung a gloved hand toward a little bush to keep his balance. For moments he simply glared, then, with great caution, he released his grip on the little bush, chose his footing carefully and began to descend toward Bart.

When he got down there, his shirttail was out in back, the seat of his trousers was dusty, and he raised a hand to push sweat off his face. He said, "What the hell do you think you're doing?"

Bart moved out of the underbrush. When no more than twenty feet separated them, he answered. "I told you I might ride out today. I figured you might be watching, so I let you get ahead, then came in behind you. What were you looking at in the yard?"

Walt leaned to beat dust off with his hat and stuff in his shirttail before replying. "Something is going on down there," he said, and raised up slowly, looking intently at Bart. "It's a fair distance, but sure as hell I saw Frank Mailer down there with some people beside a big old wagon. I think I've seen that wagon before."

Bart's mind was working fast. Even though the distance from the arroyo to the Holbrook yard was at least a mile, on a day as dazzlingly clear as this one, it was entirely possible for a man with good eyesight to make out details.

He did not doubt that Walt had seen Frank Mailer. There was an excellent chance that Mailer was with the emigrants at their wagon.

He considered the posseman. Walt was armed, Bart was not. Walt was older and not as muscular as Bart was, but he had the use of both arms. Bart strolled a little closer, halted, and shoved his hat back as he said, "Your horse is loose," and the moment the older man instinctively turned, responding to the inherent dread all rangemen had of being set afoot in open country, Bart took two long steps closer and swung his left fist. It was an awkward strike and under almost any other circumstances it would not have landed solidly, but this time it did. Walt was struck along the slant of the jaw on the right side of his head as he was turning back toward his assailant. He was tumbled backward into some bushes and, although temporarily stunned, was still conscious enough to scrabble among the supple little green limbs for a handhold to help him to regain his footing.

Bart reached him quickly, lifted the old six-shooter, and trained it on Walt. "Get up," Bart said, "and walk back to your horse. I can't take a chance on you."

Walt gingerly felt his jaw without moving. Then he stood

up and turned to go toward the tethered bay horse. "That was Mailer, wasn't it?"

Bart did not reply. When they reached the horse, he told Walt to untie it and lead it northward until they got up where Bart had left the big bay gelding.

Walt made another remark. "You was lying to me all along. You knew where Mailer was."

This time he got a response. "I didn't lie to you. You wanted to know where I'd hid him. I told you the truth; I didn't hide him."

"But you knew wnere he was."

The big bay horse was watching their approach with his head raised, his interest on the other bay horse and not on the men.

Bart made Walt remain on the ground until he could mount up, then allowed the prisoner to also get astride. As they turned toward the narrow little deer trail, Walt asked another question. "Now what? Where are we going?"

Bart withheld his answer until they were back atop the higher ground. "Turn south and head for the yard," he ordered. "I can't turn you loose, Walt."

The posseman punched a cud into his cheek and spat before replying. "All right. And I'll tell you something, horse-breaker. Jess didn't trust you from the start, and he wasn't fooled none by that pretty lady. He'll find Mailer's sign, and I'll lay you five-to-one odds that before nightfall he'll come riding into that yard yonder . . . Is that the Holbrook ranch?"

Again Bart did not answer. He was looking past his prisoner in the direction of the yard. Several people down there near the emigrant wagon had seen the pair of horsemen approaching from the north and for a short while they were motionless as they watched, then one of them turned away and hurried in the direction of the main house.

Bart groaned to himself. What he had done was get himself, and the others, between a rock and a hard place. It was certain that Deputy Morris would miss his rider. But when Walt said he had seen Frank Mailer in the Holbrook yard, there was nothing Bart could do except prevent Walt from sharing that bit of information with the deputy from Wyoming.

CHAPTER 12

The Men from Stillwater

When they halted beside the old emigrant wagon in front of the barn, Frank Mailer, Nan Holbrook, and her father were among the people looking quizzically at them. No one knew the Stillwater liveryman, but Walt recognized Mailer at once, even without his beard, and glared at him as he swung to the ground to tie his horse.

Bart took Nan and her father to one side to explain who Walt was and why he had brought him into the yard as a captive. Nan nodded in sympathetic understanding, but her father scowled at Bart. "That deputy sheriff will miss him and—"

"That deputy sheriff," interrupted Bart, "is going to pick up Mailer's tracks anyway. Morris didn't go to Holtville. As soon as Nan left him, he turned north to quarter the country until he picked up Mailer's sign. According to Walt, the deputy sheriff will most likely ride into your yard late today. John, if I'd turned this man loose he'd have hunted up the deputy and brought him down here a lot sooner."

Frank Mailer strolled over to listen. When Bart finished speaking, Mailer said, "I have a feeling I've seen that man before."

Bart nodded. "Possibly. He said he is a liveryman up at Stillwater. He's one of the deputy's posse-riders."

Mailer turned slowly to gaze back where Walt was leaning on the tie rack near his horse. Holbrook's riders were nearby and the emigrant man, who had recognized Walt as being part of that posse that had come to his camp in the foothills, was talking to his wife. The baby was sleeping up at the main house.

Mailer turned back toward John Holbrook. "Well, if one was that close, the others can't be far away."

Holbrook, who had been standing in scowling concentration, called one of his riders. "Charley, chain that man to one of the uprights in the bunkhouse."

Two Holbrook riders herded the bleak-faced, wiry older man in the direction of the log bunkhouse.

Holbrook watched until they had all disappeared inside, then he went over to his other riders and said, "Saddle up and ride north. Scatter out; keep an eye open for three strangers. Wait until Charley and Red are finished in the bunkhouse, then take them with you."

A pale, taffy-haired cowboy had a question. "And if we see them, what do we do about it?"

Holbrook seemed to need a moment to consider his reply. "Ride up and throw down on them, then fetch them to the yard. One of them is wearing a deputy sheriff's badge . . . Most of all, be careful. It'll be better if you can take them without any shooting."

An older rider put a troubled look upon his employer and said, "A lawman, Mr. Holbrook? I don't have much stomach for shooting a deputy sheriff."

"There won't be any shooting if you get right up to them before you throw down, Amos. Anyway, he's from Wyoming, which means his badge doesn't carry any weight in Colorado."

The older man did not look entirely placated, but when

the other two riders emerged from the bunkhouse heading toward the barn, he shrugged.

Bart sauntered over to where Holbrook was standing. "I'll go along," he told John Holbrook, and got a thoughtful, speculative stare from the older man. "It'll beef up the odds," Bart explained, "and Deputy Morris knows me."

Holbrook nodded and turned away. The riders followed the man called Charley into the barn for mounts, and Bart untied the big bay horse and stood at his head, waiting.

Nan, Frank Mailer, and John Holbrook were talking over near the corner of the barn, which left the emigrants standing in limbo until Nan went over to take them toward the main house. That left her father and the doctor in conversation as the riders emerged from the barn leading horses. Bart swung back across the big bay horse and reined around to go northward out of the yard with the other riders. Finally, then, Holbrook and Mailer strolled in the wake of Nan and the emigrants toward the main house.

When Bart was a mile out, the big, rawboned man named Charley eased up to ride stirrup and ask about Walt. Bart told him who Walt was and how he had caught him. The other riders crowded in to listen as Charley then asked why there were Wyoming possemen on Holbrook range, and the difficulty of answering this question kept Bart silent until he had ridden about a hundred yards—then he told them that those Wyoming manhunters were searching for that bank robber who had blown the safe of the Stillwater bank.

Charley rode with both hands lying atop his saddle horn. After a few yards he said, "All right. We've heard about that. But what the hell did you bring that fellow into our yard for, and why did Mr. Holbrook tell us to chain him? Are they after the boss?"

Bart sighed. "They're after Dr. Mailer."

The four rangemen stared. "Mailer?" exclaimed Charley. "Did he rob that bank?"

Bart shifted position slightly in the saddle and watched his horse's little ears. "He robbed the bank. He took back money that had been stolen from him by the banker up there."

That brought on another long period of silence among the rangemen, then Charley said, "All right. Red—you, Amos, and Cutter ride east, spread out, and keep watch. Bart and I'll spread out northwest. Red, if you see them—"

"I'll fire off a shot to let you know."

Charley looked pained. "No, dammit, don't fire a shot, or you're going to spook them, and they'll know something is going on."

Amos frowned. "How, then?"

"If you see them, ride west. We'll be watching for you. But don't spook them."

Charley, who had been riding for John Holbrook a number of years and knew the range better than most men, settled thoughtfully against his cantle studying the territory all the way to the far foothills. Bart offered a suggestion.

"Somewhere out here there are tracks of a man leading a lame horse. Mailer made them a few days back when he came toward your yard. The possemen are up north looking for Mailer's tracks. If we do the same thing from down here, if we can find the sign of a man on foot leading a limping horse, then go up the back trail . . ."

Charley's long-jawed face widened into a grin. He looked at the men riding behind him. "Never mind looking for the possemen, spread out and find the tracks Bart is talking about."

The sun was high; there was heat building up. Toward the distant mountains there was a bluish haze thrown back from the tiers of forest that climbed steadily toward the nearest topout.

Bart, who also knew this territory, and who had the added advantage of having an idea of the route Frank Mailer had probably used on his way south from the foothills, took

Charley with him on an angling course west and north of the Holbrook yard.

But Charley also had an advantage: He was a good sign-reader. He had been hunting cattle and horses most of his life by their tracks, even fairly old tracks on hard ground covered with buffalo grass.

He had been a wild-horse hunter for several years prior to hiring on with John Holbrook. He was the one who eventually whistled to Bart, who was a short distance away. Charley pointed with a gloved hand toward a bare place between clumps of grass where shod-horse marks were visible, with boot marks ahead of them.

Bart dismounted for a closer inspection, but Charley remained in the saddle tracing out in his mind's eye the probable direction from which those tracks had come. When Bart started bird-dogging his way from imprint to imprint, Charley rode along for a short distance, then said, "Northwest, Bart. They come from up yonder near the chewed-up place about a mile from here—that's a prairie-dog village."

They rode to that site and halted to consider the area of mounds and burrows. It covered about two acres. Prairie-dog villages were anathema to stockmen. Because there were usually hundreds of the little varmints living in each village, shooting them was out of the question. The customary method of eliminating them was to push spoonfuls of poison grain down their holes.

It never entirely eliminated the creatures, but it would nearly depopulate each village. And if the survivors did not abandon the village, most of the holes and runways would collapse after a winter or two, resulting in fewer broken legs among horses and cattle that used the same range.

Charley wagged his head. This particular village had been slated for attention before the summer was over, but recently there had been too much other work to be done.

They found where Mailer's horse had crossed and where

a runway had collapsed under his weight, pitching him in a headlong fall that must have thrown his rider. Charley said, "It wouldn't have happened in daylight." Bart nodded in agreement while gazing at the churned ground and the indications that showed clearly in dust and barren ground where a man wearing boots had got the horse back to its feet and had then led it the rest of the way across the site to better ground.

The horse was not putting much weight on his right foreleg. His tracks showed three good marks and one very light one. "Damned lucky he didn't break his leg," Charley observed.

Beyond the prairie-dog town northward where they circled around to pick up the sign, it was more difficult to read sign because of the grass, which was much thicker up there, and although Mailer's passage had pressed it down, after almost a week the grass had recovered and if it had not been for Charley's sharp eyes, they might have had to end their search right there. But he poked along slowly, occasionally backtracking to pick up the sign, then going forward again.

Neither man was conscious of the passage of time, but the sun was slanting away before Charley finally halted, no longer studying the ground, but sitting his saddle like an Indian.

He raised a gloved hand and pointed. Bart saw the possemen, too, finally, and from their behavior had no doubt what he was looking at. They were riding far apart but abreast of one another, obviously reading sign, and there were three of them.

They had not seen Bart or Charley, but they would in time because there was not a shred of cover for miles in any direction. Charley raised his eyebrows. Bart nodded at the unasked question. "It's them," he said.

Charley leaned to expectorate, then straightened up

saying, "No sign of the others behind us. What do you think about the odds?"

Bart turned the question back. "What do *you* think about them?"

"I've seen worse," he replied. "It would help if they didn't know who you were. Two strangers could ride up to them without causing any worry."

That was true; on the other hand, although the possemen would recognize Bart and despite what Walt had said about Jess Morris being suspicious of him, Morris did not actually know anything.

Charley looked around. "Where is your six-gun?"

"Hanging on the back of the kitchen door over at my claim . . . It'd be better if it didn't come to that, Charley."

The rawboned, tall man grunted a dry reply. "Yeah." Then he said, "They've seen us."

By this time because Bart could distinguish which of the trackers was Jess Morris, he assumed Morris could also recognize him. As he lifted his left hand with the reins in it, he said, "All we can do is try," and nudged the bay horse over into a walk.

The possemen closed up on Bart. Not a hand was raised in the customary range salute and not a word was spoken until the two parties were close enough for Bart and Charley to draw rein. Then Jess Morris ignored the rawboned man and looked stonily at Bart as he said, "Where is Walt?"

"Why should I know; he's your man, not mine."

"Because," replied the burly, hard-faced man, "he was at your yard last night, and he was to meet us out here somewhere this morning, and we haven't seen hide nor hair of him . . . What happened to him, Templeton?"

"He ate supper with me last night. slept in the barn, and headed out after sunup this morning."

Morris rested both hands atop the saddle horn and leaned forward slightly. "You're plumb sure of that, are you?"

Bart had no trouble returning the older man's bleak stare, because he had told the truth. Not all the truth, but the truth up to a point nevertheless. "I'm sure of it. Deputy Morris, this here is Charley Lord, range-boss for John Holbrook, whose land you are on right this minute. Charley, this is Deputy Sheriff Jess Morris out of Stillwater, Wyoming."

Charley nodded but made no move to remove a glove and offer his hand. Morris reacted the same way, with a curt nod and nothing else.

Bart looked at the other two possemen behind Morris. Both wore sidearms and had Winchesters slung from saddleboots under their saddle-fenders. They looked coldly back at Bart; like the deputy, they were clearly suspicious of him.

Morris pointed earthward. "Mailer come down this way." He replaced the gloved hand atop his saddle horn and turned his gaze toward Holbrook's range-boss. "You're foreman of this ranch we're riding on, Lord?"

Charley nodded.

"Seen any strangers lately? The man we're looking for would have been leading a limping horse. He robbed the Stillwater bank two or three weeks ago and come south. He's got eleven thousand dollars in greenbacks with him."

Charley slowly turned his head from side to side in a negative manner without taking his eyes off Morris's face. "We don't get many strangers out here," he said, "and we like it that way."

Bart looked steadily at Jess Morris. That had not been much of a description he had given of the bank robber.

CHAPTER 13

One Man's Principles

The men sitting horses behind Deputy Morris fidgeted a little. Far back, riding at a steady walk, was a solitary horseman. If Morris saw him, too, he gave no indication of it. He was studying Bart again.

"Templeton, you're getting in our way. I hope nothing bad has happened to Walt."

The approaching horseman raised his mount over into a lope and covered the intervening distance rapidly. He was one of Holbrook's riders. Bart was relieved. The odds were better now. The rider was armed. Charley turned to him and said, "Go find Red and bring him over here." After the cowboy had turned away in a lope, Charley addressed the Wyoming lawman. "Mr. Morris, my boss don't take kindly to trespassers."

The burly man's answer was softly given and did not match the hard look in his eyes. "Don't he? Well now, if he owns a big ranch, I'd guess he's wise enough to know better than to buck the law."

Charley's retort was brusque. "You're not the law."

"What the hell do you think this badge stands for, Lord?"

"I think it stands for the law up around Stillwater in Wyoming, and you're in Colorado trespassing on land where you're not welcome." Charley leaned forward in his saddle. "I'll give you some advice, Mr. Morris: You make trouble down here, and you'll regret it. If I was in your boots, I'd turn that horse around, and I wouldn't even look back until I was off Holbrook land."

Jess Morris had never impressed Bart Templeton as a man who gave ground. He did not give it now. He sat staring defiantly at the Holbrook range-boss, and when the hostile silence had run on for several moments, Bart broke it by saying, "You know where Holtville is, Deputy. Go down there, and maybe the marshal will help you. He's got the authority that you don't have."

Morris glared at Bart. "Sixty miles down and back? Where would you have Frank Mailer by the time I got back? On a fresh horse, two-thirds of the way to Mexico?"

Bart did not respond; Charley did. "You'd have to gamble on that, wouldn't you? And if we have Mailer and did as you just said, you could still nail him; circle around Holbrook range, pick up his tracks, and shag him until you could catch him in a night camp. Then sneak up in the dark and put your gun barrel in his ear."

Morris's mouth pulled down. "You just the same as admitted that you know where he is, Lord. Now I'll suggest something to you. We'll ride back to your yard with you, and I'll talk to Mr. Holbrook."

A mile or more to the rear a banner of dust was rising behind several horsemen, and while neither Bart nor Charley could see it because they were facing the posse-men, Deputy Morris and his companions saw it over the shoulders of Bart and Charley. Morris smiled at the range-boss. "The rest of your crew is coming."

Charley looked over his shoulder, then turned, and said to Morris, "You boys ready to ride back and meet them on the way to the ranch?"

Morris was agreeable. It had been his suggestion anyway so he glanced at his possemen, nodded at them and raised his rein-hand to urge his horse past Bart and Charley.

A half mile along they met the other man who had been scouring for tracks to the west. He glowered at the man with the badge on his shirt but said nothing. He turned in after Bart, Charley, and the deputy sheriff had ridden past, looked inquiringly into the face of another Holbrook rider, and was given a curt explanation of what had occurred.

Morris's Wyoming riders had wooden faces and made no attempt to strike up conversations as they rode along, and the Holbrook riders behaved the same way. It was Jess Morris up front with Charley and Bart who kept a little conversation alive. He was convinced Bart knew where his missing posseman was. Bart reiterated what he had said earlier, that Walt had left his yard about sunup this morning riding north and east.

Morris finally had to abandon the discussion because in the face of Bart's stubborn resolve he was getting nowhere, so he turned the conversation back to the fugitive and this time Charley had something to say.

"Whose money was that he took from the bank, Deputy?"

Morris stared at the tall, rawboned man. An inquiry like that indicated that Charley Lord knew quite a bit about Frank Mailer. Morris said, "Money is money when someone dynamites a bank vault to take it. A man can't just dynamite a bank safe, even if it is his money inside the thing."

That reply seemed to settle whatever doubts were in the range-boss's mind because as he rode along he turned a sardonic look upon the lawman. "You got some bad laws up in Wyoming, Deputy."

Morris's eyes narrowed. "You speaking from experience, Lord?"

Charley faced forward and did not reply. That seemed to

encourage Morris because he pursued the topic of Charley Lord having been in trouble in Wyoming. "How long since you been in Wyoming, range-boss?"

Charley continued to look impassively ahead and was slow to answer. "A long time. About fifteen years. I was pretty young back then."

"Run into the law, did you, Lord?"

"No, the law run into me."

"Care to talk about it?"

Charley finally turned to face the man riding beside him. "No, I don't think so."

Jess Morris had to be satisfied with that since it was obvious that the Holbrook range-boss was not a man who could be drawn out if he chose not to be.

Morris rode in silence from here on until they were in sight of the yard. He had tried to work Charley Lord and Bart Templeton into some kind of self-incriminating admissions and had failed. There was nothing left to talk about.

Bart's judgment of Jess Morris was simply that whatever the man was focused on got his full and unwavering attention. He was clearly a man who would never give up pursuit of an objective.

Bart did not dislike Morris, any more than he disliked Walt. The only thing he and the two had in common was Frank Mailer, and on that issue they served opposite sides.

When the Holbrook rooftops were in sight, the deputy sheriff began fishing for information about John Holbrook. All he got from Charley was a terse "Wait and see." From Bart he did not even get that much.

The emigrant wagon had been parked on the north side of the barn, between the barn and the wagon shed. There was no room for it in the shed; it was too large. The big harness horses had been turned loose and were grazing side by side less than a half mile from the yard. Like many such horses, they were big, docile animals—dependent upon people for their welfare, and they knew it—and because of that, they seldom went beyond the areas where human beings congregated.

Morris recognized the horses before they reached the yard. He also recognized the big old wagon.

As the party of horsemen entered the yard from the northwest, not a soul appeared to greet them. Bart was confident that their approach had been noted, however.

The range-riders halted at the tie rack in front of the barn and told the possemen to get down, then everyone led their animals into the barn to be unsaddled and cared for. It was during this period that Emory Wilton, the emigrant, appeared in the barn doorway, gaunt, faded, and impassive. When Jess Morris saw him, he nodded but said nothing. The emigrant nodded back.

Charley left the others on his way to the main house. Bart and the Holbrook riders herded the possemen out front and kept them there until Charley returned, looking bleak. He eyed Morris's companions as he said, "Take 'em to the bunkhouse and sit guard on them. Morris, you and Bart come with me."

As Bart walked away, the riders were already beginning to herd the possemen toward the bunkhouse. Bart imagined what their expressions would be then they walked in and saw their missing friend in chains.

At the main house Nan held the door open, and Bart shot her a quick look, then glanced around the big parlor expecting to see Dr. Mailer. He was not there, only John Holbrook was, and he eyed the Wyoming deputy and pointed to a chair as he said, "Sit. You'll be Jess Morris."

The lawman nodded, removed his hat, and sat down. For an individual who had demonstrated to Bart Templeton's satisfaction that he was never at a loss for words, Morris sat looking at his host without opening his mouth. Bart did not believe Morris was intimidated by the forbidding expression of John Holbrook, and suspected that what kept Morris quiet was his interest in this older man, whose obvious authority and wealth were evident everywhere around this ranch.

Charley responded to John Holbrook's nod and went out of the room with his employer. They were not gone long. When they returned, Charley went to stand by the front door while his employer turned his straight-backed wooden chair and sat down facing Jess Morris. Holbrook said, "I would like to see your extradition papers, Mr. Morris."

The deputy put his hat carefully on the floor at his feet before settling back into his chair, eyeing the older man. Bart thought he was caught off-guard, but evidently he wasn't because Morris said, "All I can tell you about that is that before me and my possemen left Stillwater the sheriff told me he'd wrote our governor for the papers to be sent down to the governor of Colorado for signature, then the papers was to be sent to the U.S. marshal's office in Denver."

John Holbrook sat straight in his chair. "You don't have any papers, do you?" he asked.

Morris shook his head. "No, sir, not yet. It'll be up to the marshal's office to see that someone gets them to me."

"Will they know where to find you, Mr. Morris?"

The deputy offered a delayed answer to that. "I don't know. Most likely not, Mr. Holbrook, since we haven't been able to let the sheriff up in Stillwater know where tracking Mailer has led us. But we been gone a long time; by now sure as hell them papers is waiting for us somewhere."

John Holbrook inclined his head a little. "Somewhere. But you're here, Deputy, and as far as your boss or anyone else knows, you could be almost anywhere else."

Evidently Jess Morris did not like the sound of that. "They'll find us. It wouldn't surprise me if there was a federal deputy marshal over in Holtville right now."

Holbrook raised his eyebrows. "Is that so? How would

he know to go to Holtville instead of any other town in Colorado?"

Morris did not answer.

Holbrook shot Bart a glance before addressing the deputy again. "You accused Bart Templeton of hiding Mailer."

Morris also shot Bart a look, then shrugged. "He met Frank Mailer at an emigrant camp in the foothills. Then Templeton rode away, and that same night Mailer left the emigrant camp heading south."

John Holbrook said nothing for a while. Bart heard someone working in the kitchen. For a while it was so quiet in the parlor that he could also hear horses stamping down in the corrals.

Holbrook leaned forward slightly, fixing Jess Morris with an intent look. "You don't have extradition papers, you haven't cleared your actions with Colorado law, you have trespassed on land that is closed to outsiders, and you've threatened my riders." As he finished speaking, John Holbrook sat back and reached inside his shirt, withdrew a packet covered with waterproof cloth, and held it out for Morris to take. The deputy took it, instinctively hefted it for weight, but did not take his eyes off the face of the man who had handed him the packet.

Holbrook said, "There is eleven thousand dollars in that package, Deputy, and your horses are in my barn. We'll feed you and your men, then you saddle up and go back to Stillwater. Do you understand me?"

Morris finally lowered his eyes to the packet he was holding. He replied while regarding the package. "It's a good start, Mr. Holbrook. They'll be glad to get the money back up in Stillwater." His eyes arose slowly to the cowman's face, as hard as steel. "But my job was to find Frank Mailer and bring him back. Not very much was said about the money, only that if he had it when I caught him, fetch it back too . . . Do *you* understand? I'm after an outlaw. My boys and I have nearly rode our tails off finding him. My job, pure and simple, is to apprehend a bank robber and return him up north to be tried." As he finished speaking, Jess Morris shoved the waterproof packet inside his shirt and never once let his gaze wander from the face of John Holbrook, sitting opposite him. "Now I'd like to ask you a question, Mr. Holbrook: Where is he?"

Over at the door the range-boss shifted his stance, which was the first move he had made since taking up his position at the doorway. His gaze, fixed on the deputy sheriff, was openly hostile, but he said nothing.

Neither did Bart. He had wondered whether John Holbrook could do anything with the Wyoming lawman; he had discovered several days ago that Jess Morris was both shrewd and as tough as rawhide, and now he had just discovered that Morris was also as unyielding as oak. Perhaps he should already have guessed this; he and the deputy'd had words in Bart's yard, and Morris had shown no indication of a yielding disposition over there or a couple of hours earlier out on the range.

Nan appeared in the doorway. She stood a moment, considering each man separately, then said dinner would be ready directly and asked if anyone would care for coffee to tide them over.

Bart did not believe her appearance at that particular moment was an accident. If her intention had been to get the men jarred off-center, it worked. Even Charley said he would like a cup of coffee.

CHAPTER 14

Crosscurrents

It was not a particularly unpleasant meal, but no one was relaxed. Bart speculated about the possemen down at the bunkhouse. Undoubtedly they would be fed over at the cookhouse along with Holbrook's riders.

Nan did not dine with them; she hovered to make certain their cups were kept full and the platters of food were replenished. Once or twice Jess Morris looked up at her. When she either turned away or ignored his stare, he turned his attention to her father, who was sitting in another of those straight-backed wooden chairs.

"You're going to get into trouble," he told the cowman and got back a dry response to that.

"It's happened before, Mr. Morris, but this time I kind of doubt it. Sixty miles from a settlement . . ." John Holbrook paused to fix the lawman with a saturnine smile. "I been the law out here for many years. I'm still the law out here. If you want to come right down to it, Mr. Morris, I got more authority out here than you have or anyone else."

The deputy sheriff finished his meal and pushed the empty coffee cup aside. "Range law," he told John

Holbrook, "stopped being the law twenty-five years ago, when we got courts and judges and lawyers out here."

Holbrook smiled again. "Not out here, it hasn't stopped being the law. Tell me something, Mr. Morris: Do you believe that up in Wyoming sixty miles or so from a town, when a cowman catches a cow or horse thief he takes him to a settlement?" Holbrook slowly wagged his head in reply to his own question. "I don't think so."

Jess Morris waited until Nan had removed his empty plate and cup, then said, "I know. I've run across a few unmarked graves on the far range up in our country. And Wyoming law doesn't go around digging them up to see if they got rope marks around their gullets. But this is different. I represent the law, and I'm willing to bet my pay for a year that you know where Frank Mailer is. He's a fugitive, and sure as hell, you are hiding him. That is obstructing the law, no matter whether it happens down here or up in Wyoming."

John Holbrook ignored Morris and turned to Bart. "How did the big bay horse go today?" he asked.

Bart had no complaints. "Fine. Went right along. I thought he'd do something, but he behaved himself real well."

Holbrook finished eating and reached for his coffee cup. As he raised it, he looked steadily over the rim of the cup at Jess Morris. "One of your riders is chained in my bunkhouse," he said.

Morris's brows shot up, and he turned a quick look at Bart. ". . . Walt?"

Bart nodded his head.

Holbrook went on speaking. "There is plenty of room at the bunkhouse, Deputy. You and your men can bed down there tonight."

Morris arose slowly. "That's right hospitable of you," he told Holbrook. "And we're obliged to you for being fed and all." Morris's eyes narrowed. "But we're not riding out tomorrow until someone around here tells us where Mailer is.''

Bart expected Holbrook's face to redden over this clear challenge. Instead, John sat very erect in his chair eyeing the deputy sheriff as he said, "Tomorrow is Wednesday.''

Jess Morris, who probably did not know what day of the week it was, simply gazed at the seated older man without much interest until Holbrook also said, "Tomorrow, Mr. Morris, is a sort of special day around here. Lay over, and your horses will get some rest, but you're not going to learn very much about Mailer or anything else.'' Holbrook arose and from across the table continued to regard the deputy. "Maybe, if you went down to Holtville . . .''

Morris shook his head. He'd been offered this suggestion before and had refused to consider it. "Think things over tonight,'' he told Holbrook. "Maybe by morning you'll see things differently. I don't want to get you or anyone else in trouble. I just want my prisoner.''

"He's not your prisoner,'' exclaimed Holbrook, finally beginning to show temper. "As for someone like you getting me into trouble in my own territory—go ahead and try it.''

John Holbrook left the room, and Bart escorted the Wyoming deputy out to the front veranda where lights shone from two buildings—the cookhouse and the bunkhouse. Morris paused out there to look at his companion. "Tough old cuss, isn't he?''

Bart smiled. "He didn't put this ranch together by being timid. You care for some advice?''

Morris looked at Bart. "One thing I'll always remember the Blue Basin country for, horse-breaker, is everyone's willingness to give advice. I was never in a country so full of advice-givers before in my life. . . . No, I don't want your damned advice. All I want is my prisoner. I got the money he stole, now I want *him*.'' Morris eyed the lighted bunkhouse. "Looks like maybe they got a poker session going down there," he said, and left the porch on his way through darkness across the yard in the direction of the bunkhouse.

Bart stepped to a porch upright and leaned on it. He heard a slight noise and turned to see Nan Holbrook's pale face in the gloom.

She came up and leaned on the railing, also regarding the bunkhouse. "He is an infuriating man, Bart."

He could have agreed; instead he said, "Where is Mailer?"

"With the Wiltons in one of the back bedrooms. I took supper to them before I fed the rest of you." She straightened up and looked at him. "What's been worrying me is that Dr. Mailer can hardly be free of anxiety and worry, knowing those Wyoming possemen are here in the yard. That will probably have some influence on what he has to do tomorrow morning."

Bart disagreed. "If you mean he might make a mistake, Nan, I don't think you have judged Frank Mailer right. To me, he is a thoroughly competent, experienced, and self-assured individual. I had some doubts about him, but only because I did not know him as well a few days ago as I know him now. I doubt that if the whole U.S. Army was in your yard waiting to get its hands on him tomorrow, it would keep him from concentrating on the operation."

She let go a long sigh. "You are what I need, Bart—reassurance." She smiled, then looked back where Morris had just gone. "Are you going to bed down at the bunkhouse too?"

"No. I'm going home to do my chores, but I'll be back about sunup. Walk down to the barn with me."

She walked at his left side. Because he thought she needed it, he grasped her hand and gave her fingers a squeeze. She squeezed back.

The big bay horse was drowsing on a full stomach and

did not react with pleasure at being awakened and led up to be saddled, but he did not misbehave, either. Nan watched the horse being rigged out by its one-armed owner and voiced misgivings.

"Why don't you take one of our horses, Bart? Have you ever ridden him in the dark?"

Bart finished cinching up and eased the stirrup back down as he smiled across the saddle at her. "No, I never have, but he didn't make a mistake today. I don't believe he will tonight. Thanks, just the same."

He led the horse out back to be mounted and when she came close, he stopped to face her. "That was a good supper."

She smiled at him. "I'm glad you liked it."

He groped for something to prolong this moment and came up with a question. "How is the emigrant baby?"

"All right. Dr. Mailer said what it needed was something besides a drafty wagon to sleep in, and quiet. Last night he thought it might be developing the croup, but this morning he told me its breathing was fine." Nan turned slightly at the sound of raucous laughter from the bunkhouse. "I wish they weren't here," she said, about the possemen.

He turned the bay horse, toed in, and swung up. For a moment the bay horse held his head high and had a hump under the saddle, then that moment passed as Bart said "I'll be back in time for hotcakes" and rode away.

It was a pleasant night, but part of the heavens to the northeast seemed to be obscured by clouds—at least Bart could discern no stars in that direction. It was possible another storm was moving in. He settled forward in the saddle, hoping the weather would hold at least until tomorrow night, and concentrated on riding.

Bart thought about Jess Morris, speculating that if someone had explained to him why John Holbrook was being so obdurate Morris might have slackened off a little on his stand. But today for the first time he'd had a strange feeling about Morris.

They were almost to the yard when the bay horse flung up his head, staring dead ahead, his ears errect.

Bart slackened a little in the saddle. The animal's quick sense of interest in something did not necessarily mean trouble. On the other hand, when he'd reacted in an identical manner earlier this same day, Bart had found Walt.

The yard was dark, as were the buildings. When Bart crossed to the front of the barn, he turned to peer at the porch of his house; that had been where Walt had been waiting last night.

This time, however, there was no one on the porch.

He dismounted at the tie rack and looped his reins before stepping to the left side of the horse to place the stirrup over the saddle-seat before loosening the latigo so that he could lift off the saddle. Suddenly two men walked out from inside the barn.

The larger of the men had a badge on his coat, which was hardly visible in starlight. The second man was not as thick, not as tall. Bart recognized this man first; it was one of John Holbrook's riders. The man beside him was Jack Kennedy, the town marshal of Holtville. He and Bart were acquaintances, nothing more.

Marshal Kennedy skipped the preliminaries and said, "You just come from the Holbrook place?"

Bart shouldered the saddle with one arm and started for the saddle-pole inside the barn. He answered as he walked past the big man. "Yeah."

Kennedy and the cowboy followed him inside and leaned in the doorway, where poor visibility made it seem best to wait until Bart had flung the saddle across the pole. When Bart started toward them to lead his horse out back to the round corral, the Holtville marshal had another question for him. "Who is over there?"

Bart unlooped the reins, then paused to answer before leading the horse away. "Four Wyoming passemen, the

Holbrooks, their riders, and an emigrant couple named Wilton with their baby."

Marshal Kennedy waited until Bart was leading the horse away before speaking again. "Anyone else?"

Bart corralled the horse, latched the gate, and turned to face his two visitors. He eyed the lawman particularly. "I thought you were going to ride to the Holbrook place."

Jack Kennedy eased his considerable heft against the corral before replying. "I was. Tim here said his boss wanted to see me, but when we got close enough to see the yard, we could see some strangers—and you. I figured I'd ride on over to your place and when you come home get the information from you. Those possemen—they're after that bank robber from up at Stillwater?"

"Yes."

"Then, why are they hanging around the Holbrook place; is that outlaw holed up over there, Bart?"

Bart straightened up. "Let's go in the house and get some coffee; it's getting chilly out."

He needed time. The two men followed him across the yard. Inside the house, he lighted the lamp and led them to the kitchen, where he got a fire going in the stove and put his coffeepot atop one of the burners. Then they all three sat down at the table, the town marshal intently studying his host.

He asked the question again. "Is that bank robber holed up over at the Holbrook place?"

Bart watched the cowboy roll and light a smoke before answering. "The Wyoming deputy doesn't have extradition papers, Marshal. If he catches Mailer, he won't have any authority to take him out of Colorado."

Marshal Kennedy considered that for a moment, and meanwhile Bart got three cups and put them on the table in front of his guests. "How do you know he doesn't have extradition papers?" Kennedy asked.

"Because he admitted it when he talked to John Holbrook."

Kennedy relaxed and sprawled in his chair. The kitchen was getting warm, and although the coffee had not yet begun to boil, it was getting hot and its aroma filled the room. Kennedy looked at the cowboy. "I was right. If we'd ridden into the yard we'd have landed right in the middle of a mess I wouldn't have had any ideas about. I was right to come over here and wait." Having said that, the marshal turned his attention back to Bart.

"Once more: Is Frank Mailer over there?"

"Yes," replied Bart. He settled in to tell the marshal who Mailer was, why he had robbed the Stillwater bank, what he had done for the emigrants and what he intended to do for John Holbrook first thing in the morning. He concluded by mentioning again Deputy Morris's lack of authority down in Colorado.

Marshal Kennedy sat listening. When there was silence again, he rose to get the coffeepot and returned to the table with it.

CHAPTER 15

Discrepancies

Tim, the Holbrook range-rider, was outspoken enough to mention that neither he nor Marshal Kennedy had eaten since morning, so Bart sighed and went to his cupboard. Before this mess was finished he was going to have to hitch up and drive down to Holtville for more supplies.

He fed them, and drank coffee while they ate. The lawman was silent through most of the meal, but once he looked up to say, "Hell, if I'd known I was going to ride into a hornet's nest out here I'd have rounded up a posse."

A little later he made another comment. "I don't look forward to bucking John Holbrook."

Bart and the cowboy said nothing. When the meal was finished, Bart's visitors helped him clean up the kitchen, which the Wyoming posseman had not done. Then Jack Kennedy built a smoke and lighted it. He went out onto the front porch to smoke because his wife of twenty-seven years had broken him of smoking in the house, and old habits were the strongest ones.

Kennedy considered bedding down here and waiting for dawn to ride over to John Holbrook's place. But it might be better if he went over there tonight, late as it was. Not because he was eager to get involved, but because with everyone asleep, he and John Holbrook could sit down and talk quietly.

Marshal Kennedy was a good peacekeeper. He could handle almost any two rangemen who arrived in town on a Saturday night, but what he was facing now would most likely require something different from big, knotty fists and a cocked six-gun.

He killed the cigarette, leaned on the porch railing in troubled thought, and finally made his decision. He knew as much law as the next cow-town marshal. If the deputy from Wyoming did not have authority to take Mailer back up north with him, then Kennedy would see that he didn't take him back until he did get the authority.

Bart and Tim came out to join the marshal.

"What time in the morning do you figure to go back over there?" Kennedy asked Bart.

"I figure to leave here right after breakfast so as to reach the Holbrook place about sunup. Four o'clock, Marshal?"

Kennedy let go a rattling big sigh. "Four o'clock it will be," He looked at the cowboy. "You going to lay over or head for home?"

"Head for home," stated the rangeman, so Bart and the marshal went down to the barn while the cowboy saddled up. He told them he would let John Holbrook know the law from Holtville would be in the yard about sunup, then he left them and rode due eastward.

Kennedy and Bart returned to the porch to sit awhile. The marshal made another cigarette, dreading what he would have to do tomorrow.

"Lately," said Bart, "I've wondered a little about Deputy Morris. There's something about him I can't figure out. It's not always what he says, it's what he doesn't say."

Marshal Kennedy smoked and said nothing. His expression in the night gloom, however, did not brighten any over what he had just been told. When he leaned to stamp out the smoke a few minutes later, he said, "Four of them. I don't like that."

Bart hid a yawn before answering. "Holbrook's got four men, besides Tim. With you and me and Holbrook, the odds will be in our favor."

Kennedy looked skeptically at his host. "Looks to me like your right arm isn't much use in a sling, and Holbrook won't be able to do much if that sawbones is going to cut him open." The thought inspired the lawman to say something else. "I can't imagine old Holbrook holding still for something like that. He could end up in a chair for the rest of his life. And if I was in his boots, I'm not sure I'd want a bank robber to cut into me, even if he was a doctor back east."

Bart yawned again. This was the second night in a row he hadn't got to bed until after midnight. He stood up, adjusted his shirt around the bandaged right arm, and Marshal Kennedy took his cue from this. Bart offered him the house to unroll his blankets in, but the marshal declined and went down to the barn.

In bed, Bart stirred only once—that was when he thought he heard running horses. He raised up in pitch dark to listen, but if it had been horses, they had moved out of hearing-distance. He sat a moment, speculating about wolves chasing his brood mares and their colts, then decided it probably had not been his horses, and dropped back down to sleep until a faint hint of approaching day roused him again. This time he rolled out, dressed himself with his left hand, something he was beginning to master, then went through the house and out back to the wash-rack to scrub and shave. On the way he stirred dry kindling into the coals from last night's supper fire.

From the side-porch he had a good view of the east range and the yard. He was not surprised to see a bleak sky— thick, dark-looking clouds moving with an almost imperceptible sluggishness.

The storm he had thought was coming from the northeast last night had made good time. He stood drying his face and hands after shaving, considering the troubled heavens and thinking that if this second deluge had occurred a couple of weeks earlier, Jess Morris and his Wyoming possemen would not be in the Holbrook yard now because there would have been no tracks of a fugitive to lead them there.

Marshal Kennedy stamped noisily up to the front veranda as Bart was coddling his cooking-fire in the stove. He called, and Kennedy walked in. He had evidently washed down at the stone trough behind the barn, and he was neither smiling nor talkative as Bart set a cup of warmed-over hot coffee in front of him. The marshal accepted the coffee with a brusque nod. After emptying the cup Kennedy's attitude changed, and his expression brightened. He even said, "Good morning. You ready to go twist someone's tail?"

They finished eating before the sky had lightened very much and were on their way to Holbrook's with cold and grayness accompanying them. If Marshal Kennedy had noticed the changed weather, he said nothing about it, but he was bundled in an old coat, and occasionally he would shoot a look upward.

Bart was riding the big bay horse again. Marshal Kennedy eyed the horse with experienced eyes and a pulled-down mouth. His own animal was a seal-brown, a good animal with breeding somewhere in his bloodline, and big. He probably weighed a little over a thousand pounds, but Jack Kennedy was neither a small nor lightweight individual. He required a large horse.

About a mile out, a startled rabbit sprang from beneath a bush. The bay horse sucked sideways with surprising quickness, but Bart had seen the rabbit at the same time his horse had. He had a deep seat in the saddle, had his knees locked, and was holding up the reins so that they would be too short to permit the mustang to get his head down.

But the bay horse did not attempt to buck or run. After shying violently, he straightened up and walked steadily along. Marshal Kennedy made a tart remark. "Next time you won't see the rabbit in time, and he'll dump you on your head ten miles from home. Where did you get that horse, anyway?"

Bart told him. Kennedy nodded his head. He had thought as much. He had made a miserable living for a couple of years a long time back trapping and selling wild horses. He knew the look of a wild horse when he saw it.

"Don't ever trust one," he told Bart. "They're like mules; they'll work for you for ten years waiting for you to get careless, so's they can kick your head off."

The sun was trying to force passage through a wedge of heady clouds on the horizon. Bart and his companion were more than halfway to their destination when Bart mentioned thinking he had heard running horses last night.

Marshal Kennedy had also heard them. "Going from the northeast to the west like something was chasing them." He looked from beneath his pulled-down hatbrim. "You got wolves out here, Bart?"

"Yes."

Kennedy wagged his head. "You ought to take a few days off and go hunt those varmints down."

"I will when I get a little time. Right now I got something else on my mind." He raised his left arm to gesture with. "Holbrook's buildings."

The marshal regarded the buildings with grave interest. This was not his first trip out here, but because of the distance, he did not come out often. In fact, the last time he had been in the Holbrook yard was four years earlier when he and a couple of friends from town had been elk hunting.

While Kennedy was looking toward the yard from about a mile away, Bart repeated what Jess Morris had told him about the U.S. Marshal's office up in Denver, and Kennedy brought his attention around to the speaker slowly.

"Maybe," the marshal said with doubt in his voice. "But I'd say unless it was federal money Mailer took from the bank, the U.S. Marshal wouldn't be involved. I've handled a lot of extraditions in my time and only once, when some fellows stole an army payroll, was the U.S. Marshal called in. The way those things usually work is that if the governor of Wyoming puts in an extradition request to the governor of some other state, in this case Colorado, it goes directly to the governor's office. If he agrees to an extradition, and they usually do, why, then someone mails me a copy of the extradition order and sends another copy to the law in Wyoming who'll come down here to catch the fugitive and take him back to Wyoming."

Bart rode in silence for a short distance. This was not the sequence Jess Morris had explained to him. According to Morris, the order would come through the U.S. Marshal's office. Either the deputy sheriff from Stillwater did not know what he was talking about or else he had been putting up a good front to cover the face that he had no extradition order.

Bart turned with a frown toward Marshal Kennedy. "That's not the way Morris explained it to me, Jack."

Kennedy was looking toward the yard again and answered without enthusiasm. "I'll talk to the deputy," he said, and lapsed into silence. He seemed interested in the fact that at this time of morning when there should have been activity in a ranch-yard, the Holbrook yard was empty; there were no men visible in the barn area or out back at the corrals, where normally someone would be pitching feed to the using horses. There was no smoke rising from the cookshack stovepipe, and over at the main house only one lamp glowed in the parlor behind the front big window.

Kennedy rode up to the working corrals behind the barn before reining to a halt. He studied the big yard, its buildings, and finally muttered under his breath to the effect that he did not like what he saw.

Bart, too, was beginning to wonder and worry. There should have been smoke rising above the bunkhouse, too, and from the kitchen stovepipe over at the main house. He slackened his reins and sat with Marshal Kennedy until a dog barked somewhere across the yard in the direction of the shoeing shed, then Bart raised his rein-hand.

Riding into the yard from behind the barn, their horses made the only sounds. When they turned in at the tie rack out front and swung down, they were even more aware of the ranch's air of abandonment. While Kennedy was looping his reins and glancing toward the main house, that dog barked again, louder this time.

Jack Kennedy straightened up, pulling loose the tie-down over his holstered Colt. Bart was staring in the direction of the cookshack. At this time of early morning not only should there have been smoke rising, but there should have been the sound of men at breakfast. He said. "Come along" to the marshal and struck out across the yard.

The cookshack was empty, the stove was cold, and it was clearly evident that no one had made preparation for breakfast. It was eerie, and Jack Kennedy went to a window to stand gazing back across the yard. "It's like something come along and swallowed everybody up," he said. He turned toward the horse-breaker. "You ever had the feeling that eyes was on your back?"

Bart did not reply. He returned to the cookshack porch and stood hesitantly. Light from the main-house window suggested that someone was over there. Without speaking to Marshal Kennedy, he walked down off the cookshack porch and started toward the main house, which was at the extreme south end of the yard, separate from the other buildings.

Kennedy caught up. He walked with his head turning from side to side. "Targets," he muttered to Bart. "We're perfect targets."

Bart's reply was curt. "We have been ever since we rode

into the yard, and so far no one's tried anything. I got a bad feeling about this, Jack."

They were passing the bunkhouse from a distance of several yards toward the center of the big yard when Bart detected a sound. He stopped and faced the bunkhouse. Kennedy stopped, too, and said, "What is it?"

"A noise from the bunkhouse."

Kennedy's scowl deepened as he surveyed the front of the bunkhouse; then he lifted out his six-gun and said, "You go up on the left side of the door. I'll go on the right side."

They separated when they reached the little bunkhouse porch. Bart was unarmed. It would not have made much difference if he had been because he couldn't shoot left-handed.

Marshal Kennedy cocked his gun, held the barrel tipped up, and gestured for Bart to lift the latch and kick the door inward.

Bart reached for the latch-rope, paused a second or two, then gave it a violent downward pull and kicked out with his right leg. The door flew open, struck something and quivered; otherwise there was not a sound.

CHAPTER 16

A Crisis

The sight Marshal Kennedy and Bart Templeton saw inside the log building was one neither of them would ever forget. There were nine people on the floor, bound and gagged. Charley, the range-boss, turned his head to stare at the men in the doorway. He and the other four Holbrook riders had empty holsters. Beyond them, Nan and her father were propped against the wall, also staring toward the door. The ranch cook, an old man with a paunch and not much hair, was lying on his back near the cold stove. There was dry blood down the side of his face from a wound atop his head. He did not move. There was another man tied and gagged, a stranger to Bart. He was tall and rangy, like the range-boss, but had light-gray eyes and an almost lipless mouth. He stared straight at Jack Kennedy and ignored Bart. He made a sound behind his gag.

Kennedy and Bart used clasp-knives to cut the ropes after which the bound people removed their own gags and the rangy, light-eyed stranger got stiffly to his feet, flexed both legs a few times, then addressed Jack Kennedy, whose badge he had stared at. With a stiff movement the rangy man dug in a pocket and held forth a big hand so that

Marshal Kennedy could see the federal deputy marshal's badge in his palm.

Jack looked up at the man with a scowl. The stranger pocketed his badge and said, "Deputy U.S. Marshal Les Slater, out of Denver."

Everyone else seemed to be speaking at once, so Slater took Kennedy's arm and steered him back outside. They were out there a long time.

Nan got two of the riders to lift the injured cook and place him on a bunk. She then went after water to wash his face and cleanse his wound. During her absence her father told Bart that when Jess Morris and his men had seen the stranger named Slater ride into the yard from the direction of Holtville, they held a council in the bunkhouse, then threw down on the ranch-riders, disarmed and trussed them, and started toward the main house where Slater and Holbrook were in conversation on the porch. The cook had seen them emerge from the bunkhouse with guns and had stepped inside for his old rifle. He had then returned to the porch and yelled for the Wyoming possemen to drop their guns. One turned and fired, and the slug dropped the cook with a crease over the top of his head. He was very lucky to be alive, Holbrook said.

Charley came over to check on the cook, who had regained consciousness. He said he had a splitting head-ache, and his eyes were bloodshot.

Now, the yard had activity. Men went to the barn to verify that indeed Deputy Morris and his possemen had gone. When Nan returned to look after the cook, Bart went back outside, followed by the range-boss. Charley wagged his head. "I never liked their looks from the time you and I found them out yonder tracking Mailer."

For the first time since entering the yard, and later during the noisy excitement after releasing the bound and gagged people, Bart thought of Frank Mailer. He had not been among the people left in the bunkhouse. He asked the range-boss what had become of him, and Charley shrugged bony shoulders. "As far as I know, they took him with them. I know they got inside the main house and forced John to open his safe and give them the money he had in it, and they tied the Wiltons. Mailer was in there too. I think they must have taken him with them."

Jack Kennedy and the deputy marshal walked over to Bart. Kennedy said, "One thing that Morris-fellow said was true. The U.S. Marshal's office is involved." He unfolded a coarse piece of paper he was holding and held it up. "Is that your Wyoming deputy sheriff, Bart?"

The likeness on the wanted dodger was unmistakable. Bart nodded his head as he read the poster. Jess Morris's name was Hugh Thompson. He was wanted for murder and robbery. He and three companions had stopped a stagecoach outside of Stillwater, Wyoming, killed the guard and took a mail pouch containing money from the Denver mint, which was being sent to a federal deposit bank down at Santa Fé in New Mexico. Bart raised his eyes to the federal deputy.

Slater smiled a little. "We've been hunting Thompson for a year, since that robbery and killing. I'll tell you how he got Jess Morris's identity and badge. Morris evidently saw a campfire in the mountains and rode toward it; he rode into the camp where Thompson and his partners were. He must have assumed they were rangemen because otherwise he would not have told them who he was and that he was chasing a fugitive named Frank Mailer who had eleven thousand dollars in cash on him.

"I found Morris's body in a canyon near their camp. If I'd been one day closer maybe I could have saved Deputy Morris's life . . . I tracked them down to a wagon-camp but the wagon was gone, heading down this way. I knew where Holtville was and headed over there. Folks told me at Holtville their town marshal had left town riding in this direction with one of the Holbrook riders. I started after them day before yesterday and rode into the yard last night.

Hugh Thompson knew me by sight. I've been after him for a year. That was all he needed last night—to recognize me when I rode into the yard.

"He already had the eleven thousand dollars from the Stillwater bank, and he probably guessed a man like John Holbrook would have a sizable amount of cash somewhere in the main house. When he recognized me Thompson and his partners headed toward the porch with their guns cocked." The federal lawman paused, looked around the yard, then said, "They went west. We could hear them go thundering out of the yard."

Jack Kennedy tapped Bart's arm. "Remember those running horses we heard last night out beyond your place?"

Bart did not reply. He remembered, but he was looking at the federal marshal. "There was a man named Frank Mailer. . . ."

Slater nodded his head. "I know. The man who robbed the Stillwater bank. Maybe he went with them, I don't know. What I do know, Mr. Templeton, is that it's going to rain and unless I can find their tracks and keep them this time, most likely they're going to get away. . . . I need someone to ride with me—right now. It would help to have someone who knows the country. I sure don't, and I doubt that Thompson does." Slater paused again, but this time without looking away from Bart. "It's been a hard year, Mr. Templeton, and this is as close as I've been to Thompson. I figure just one more real hard effort and I'll find him." Slater turned toward Jack Kennedy. "Marshal . . . ?"

Kennedy gave a quick nod as he said, "I'm ready. I'll borrow a carbine from someone. I don't like being away from town very long, but I'm ready any time you are, Slater." Jack looked steadily at Bart. "You know the country west of your place. I sure don't. And that big mustang of yours needs some hard riding."

Bart looked around and saw Nan and her father leaving the bunkhouse. He said, "All right. Go saddle up, and give me fifteen minutes . . . Jack, see if you can borrow two saddleguns. Ask the range-boss."

He overtook the Holbrooks halfway to the main house. When he told them what he, Slater, and Kennedy were about to do, John Holbrook's brows tensed. "Take a couple of my men with you, and be careful. That runty one called Walt is a good shot. He hit the cook last night in the dark firing from the hip."

Bart nodded, then he said, "Did they get much money from you safe?"

Holbrook answered curtly. "Not much. About two thousand dollars. That eleven thousand I gave Morris—uh, I mean Thompson—didn't come from Frank Mailer, it came from my safe. It was my money, not Mailer's bank loot."

Bart stared at the older man. "Where is Mailer? If he went with them—"

"He didn't go with them," Nan said. "I don't know whether they looked for him or not, but they didn't find him. There is a hidden room under the house my father built years ago when Indian attacks were common. Dr. Mailer is down there."

Bart said, "Are you sure, Nan?"

She was. "When I went after the medicine for the cook's wound I untied the Wiltons, told them what had happened this morning, then raised the trapdoor to see if Dr. Mailer was all right. He was."

Bart stood gazing at the Holbrooks. They gazed back. Whatever the rest of this gray and dismal day held could not possibly compare with what had already happened.

Jack Kennedy called from in front of the barn. He was holding the hackamore reins to the saddled mustang, and he was clearly impatient.

Nan leaned suddenly and kissed Bart on the cheek, then straightened back as she said, "Please . . . if it comes down to a matter of letting them get away or risking your life, let them get away, Bart."

He stared at her for a moment and then hurried down where Slater and Kennedy were waiting. John Holbrook took several steps back toward the center of the yard and called for his range-boss, but it was too late, Bart and his companions were already loping away from the yard. There would not be enough time for Holbrook riders to catch horses, saddle them and join the three hard-riding men.

Overhaed, the ominous clouds were thickening, blotting out what little sunlight had been able to penetrate them earlier. John Holbrook turned back toward the house with his daughter. Twice as they approached the house she turned to watch Bart and the marshals, who were growing smaller in the distance. Her father gruffly said, "He'll be careful. Anyone who breaks horses for a living doesn't take unnecessary chances. Let's get the doctor out of the cellar. We agreed to do this surgery on Wednesday and by gawd, we're going to do it!"

She frowned at her father but went obediently to the main house with him.

Over the horizon from the Holbrook place, the federal marshal rode a leggy big brown horse who had been honed down to little more than rawhide and muscle. He held to his lope seemingly without effort for three miles, until they had Bart's yard in sight on their left side.

Slater seldom looked at his companions as they rode. To Bart, it was obvious that Slater's last-chance wish to catch Thompson and his gang was what was driving him now. He had got close enough to recognize the outlaws he had been pursuing for over twelve months, and they had eluded him once again. This time he was not going to stop until he got them. Jack Kennedy was the same kind of implacable, stubborn man.

Bart rode past his buildings with little more than a glance in their direction. The trail they were following was clear; even on hard ground, four shod horses being ridden close to one another left a trail anyone could follow.

Bart saw Slater glance upward a couple of times and guessed that he was worrying about the storm. If it was a heavy downpour like the other one last month, it would wash out horse tracks. If that happened, the only way the pursuers would be able to find the outlaws would be by guesswork—and knowledge of the countryside the outlaws did not have.

Bart knew the range west of his yard. He owned some of it, the rest of it was unsettled, open country. A hard ride west there was a rise of foothills and mountains that were a continuation of the mountains north. These mountains formed an immense horseshoe shape around Blue Basin from east to west. Bart had been through those westerly mountains just once, his first year in Blue Basin when he had gone exploring. Beyond the mountains, which were about fifty miles through and rugged, with dark stands of giant fir and pine trees, was another basin, even larger than Blue Basin. It was uninhabited, or at least it had been several years ago when Bart had ridden partway across it.

He had encountered more game over there than he had ever seen in one place in his life. He had also seen a small herd of buffalo over there, something he had not expected ever to see. Buffalo were nearly extinct. Bart had never told a soul about seeing that forlorn little herd. Undoubtedly someday hunters would find them, but they would never do it from anything Bart said.

Slater pulled his leggy brown horse down to a walk. Kennedy followed his example, looped his reins, and went to work rolling a smoke. Bart's big bay was lathered, but he was not breathing hard. Slater turned and said, "Any towns?"

Bart shook his head. "Not until you get about three hundred miles west. I've never been over there. I saw the place on a map down in Holtville at the land office one time."

Kennedy trickled smoke when he said, "I've been over

there. It's called Fort Winfield. But we'll find the Thompson gang before we get that far, or we'll never find them at all." Kennedy smoked and squinted toward the distance-hazed mountains. "If they get up those foothills . . ." He stabbed out his cigarette atop the saddle horn. "Slater, as soon as we get close, they're going to see us coming, and I doubt that they'll figure we're the pony express. . . . Sure as hell if they can get into those mountains, they'll set up a bushwhack."

Les Slater faced forward studying the vast land—and a big fat raindrop landed on the back of his gloved hand. He quickly tipped his head back. A second big fat raindrop came down. This one hit him on the nose. He lowered his head and searched the distance for sign of horsemen. Bart had been doing this for the last half hour.

There were no riders in sight. In fact, there was no movement of any kind, not even browsing wild game. The range west of Bart Templeton's yard was empty, huge, and desolate.

CHAPTER 17

Weather

For more than an hour there were only those big occasional raindrops, and in that length of time the two lawmen and the horse-breaker covered about eight miles, and did it without pushing their horses.

In this kind of a pursuit if a man overrode his horse, he could easily end up on foot. Les Slater pointed toward a stand of distant trees, where the gang could be hiding. The trail they were following did not not turn in that direction, but it might another mile or so ahead.

Bart knew that place. Several years ago he had nooned there. As they rode in that general direction he kept watching, and when it was possible to make out details where the shade lingered, he saw neither horses nor men. Slater evidently had been watching, too, because he relaxed when they were parallel to the trees and shook his head. He did not speak. In fact, Bart was beginning to understand that Marshal Slater was not a talkative individual. Nor was Jack Kennedy, which left Bart with little to say to either of them unless they asked, as Les Slater did a mile beyond the stand of trees as they were approaching a wide arroyo. It bisected their route. But the trail veered northward and did not change; evidently the outlaws had not known they were being chased when they got out this far because instead of riding down into the arroyo to establish an ambush, they rode around its northern end, then angled back southward again before aiming directly west toward the mountains.

Slater shook his head. "They could have picked us off like crows on a fence from down in there."

Bart pointed. The land ahead was beginning to be more upended as they got closer to the foothills. "Plenty of other places," he told the town marshal.

Slater studied the sky again. The intermittent raindrops had not increased, but from the appearance of the sky they would eventually.

Bart took them southward away from the trail they had been following into some broken country, and when Jack Kennedy scowled about leaving the trail, Bart told him that if there was an ambush up ahead somewhere, following those tracks was going to lead them straight into the open end of someone's Winchester barrel. Whereas, if they followed their present course a mile or two, they would be not only below the outlaws, they would also be in a position to flank them.

Kennedy continued to scowl, but Les Slater seemed agreeable.

The men had to sashay gingerly back and forth because of big, jutting rocks along the way. The area they were picking their way through was also dense with trees.

It also had rattlesnakes. Bart's mustang who had matured in the wild with the ability to detect the scent of snake pulled back twice, and both times there was a rattler on the trail.

Slater wagged his head admiringly, but Jack Kennedy still viewed the big bay horse as a hazard to a rider and said so.

They came around a low, thick little hill and encountered a sluggish creek. When their shadows fell across the water, trout-minnows exploded in all directions by the hundreds. Slater said someday he would like to return to this country with camp-gear and live off trout for a few weeks.

What intrigued Bart was that the water had been a little muddy even before the fish had made it worse. Without commenting he turned northward on the far side of the creek and while utilizing the cover of creek-willows, picked his way up in the direction of those tracks they had been following.

They found an area of pressed-flat grass where men had rested recently. The imprints of hobbled horses were visible in the soft earth beside the creek.

Les Slater swung off to quarter. Jack Kennedy watered his horse, himself, then faced the mountains with a squinty-eyed look. "They've sure as hell seen us by now," he told Bart.

Raindrops made faint whispery sounds among the willows and out upon trampled grass. Slater walked back, looking unhappy. The rain was finally beginning to pelt down. The drops were smaller, but there were a lot more of them.

The clouds were moving. They were low, dark, and swollen, but they were slowly and ponderously moving southward.

When Slater swore about the rain, Bart was snugging up his saddle cinch. He was less concerned about rain washing out the sign than he was about getting drenched. He had no slicker behind his saddle. Neither did Kennedy or Slater.

Kennedy thought they should make a beeline for the timbered mountainsides. Bart disagreed. If Kennedy was correct about Morris and his partners watching them, perhaps from up that same sidehill, making a run for it wouldn't be very smart. Slater evidently concurred with this unspoken opinion. He pulled an old blanket-coat from behind his saddle and shrugged into it. The blanket-coat would not turn water, but it would slow down the drenching process.

Slater asked Bart if he knew of a place where the three of them might wait out at least the worst of the storm. Bart swung up across his saddle and sat still until the other two men were also astride, then he continued northward until they came upon the trail they had departed from an hour earlier. Bart turned toward the mountains paralleling the tracks and watching them as his bay horse plodded along, head down, resigned to a drenching.

There had been Indians throughout this area probably for centuries. The place Bart was heading for he had come upon by accident while looking for his horse on the only other time he had come this far from his yard. The horse had been hobbled, but an experienced horse could hop in hobbles faster than a man could run. His horse had browsed through underbrush from grassy place to grassy place. And he had been standing with his nose near the ground, his ears pointing forward as though he'd had a rattlesnake in front of him.

It had not been a rattlesnake, it had been a cave, where scabrous lava-rock had cooled in prehistoric times, bursting in places like giant water-bubbles. Some of the caves were extensive, but most of them were barely deep enough for three men to huddle in. He led Kennedy and Slater to a large cave with a shattered front opening that was as tall as a man atop a horse.

He dismounted, handed his reins to Kennedy, took the carbine Kennedy had borrowed back at the Holbrook place, and stepped into the opening of the cave. Kennedy said, "Be careful. We're not the only ones out here, Bart."

The horse-breaker was not worried about the outlaws having holed up in there because their tracks had bypassed this area to the north by at least half a mile.

He tried to lead his horse inside. The animal snorted and pulled back, but when Slater and Kennedy led their horses inside the big mustang followed. He was more or less indifferent to a soaking but like all horses, he instinctively did not want to be separated from other horses.

Water dripped from the overhead rock in steady streams. Now, finally, the storm was directly overhead. Rain did not come in torrents—it came in actual waves of water. The men standing inside the rock opening looked out.

Kennedy had jerky in his saddlebags. So did Slater. Bart had neither jerky nor saddlebags, so his companions shared with him. When Kennedy eventually built a smoke and lighted it, he was looking caustically out at the drowning world. "We could be holed up in here for a week," he grumbled, speaking loudly in order to be heard above the roar made by the rainfall.

Bart was not too worried. "Thompson and his friends won't be any better off," he said, "and this lava field doesn't go as far north as they were riding, so maybe they won't even have this much shelter."

Because the storm was moving slowly, and also because they were directly beneath the heart of it, it appeared for a while that Jack Kennedy's dour prediction might be proved true; they might indeed be forced to remain in the cave for a long time.

But eventually the heart of the storm bore southward. The rainfall continued but not with the same degree of force.

Kennedy smoked another cigarette and crouched in the opening, squinting out. There was nothing to see but soiled walls of lowering clouds. Still, the rainfall continued to diminish until it amounted to little more than a constant drizzle. The men could handle this. They led the horses out into a sodden, cowed world, straddled damp saddle-seats, and with Bart leading, went northward again seeking the trail of the outlaws.

As Les Slater had observed back at the Holbrook place, a rainfall would obliterate tracks. Bart could not actually find the place where he had last seen tracks. Slater, it turned out, was a good tracker. But he did not have a trail to follow, only a general direction. As he told Jack and Bart, the fugitives had been heading for the mountains before the storm, and there was no reason to think the rainfall had made them change their plans.

They rode west through a chilly drizzle that was accompanied by a wet mist, their visibility down to about a hundred yards. They rode hunched, mostly silent and uncomfortable, but nothing was mentioned about finding a place to make a fire to dry out by.

Bart's mending right arm ached a little from the cold; otherwise, he felt well enough. He looked to his left and right at his companions, looked straight ahead as far as he could see, then pulled his head down against the upturned collar of his old riding coat and thought about Nan Holbrook and her father. If Frank Mailer had kept his word about performing the surgery today, by now he should be midway through with it—or, for all Bart knew, perhaps finished with it.

He was trying to imagine what recovery would be like for Nan's father when Slater made a slight sound, raised a gloved hand, and pointed.

They were well into the foothills by this time and some distance onward there was a reddish-orange flickering glow where someone had found enough dry wood to make a fire. It looked to be about a mile ahead and slightly northward.

Jack Kennedy straightened in the saddle. "I don't think they'd be doing that if they knew we were trailing them."

It was possible that the outlaws had not detected any pursuit, but it seemed to Bart that unless they were absolute greenhorns, they should have. Unless of course the storm had hindered their rearward visibility.

Then the actual significance of that fire hit him. He said, "Slater, we're wet and miserable, that fire looks awful good—and if they're up there beside it, I'll buy you a new Stetson hat."

Bart's implication seemed to influence both lawmen at the same time, and Jack Kennedy whose opinion had been that the outlaws were indeed around their fire because they did not know how close pursuers were, now changed his mind. "I told you fellows miles back they'd set up a bushwhack."

Les Slater did not say a word. He rode along squinting at the fire for a fair distance, then halted. When his companions also drew rein, Slater said, "All right, you two gents swing wide southward, and I'll go wide northward—and keep going past the fire toward the mountains. When you figure you're maybe a mile or so beyond the fire, turn northward and I'll be turning southward. Then, gents, we'll start back down toward their fire from in back. With some luck we ought to be able to come up behind them." Slater gazed from Bart to Jack Kennedy. "The best way to handle an ambush is to sneak around the bushwhackers and turn it around on them. All right?"

Neither Bart nor the Holtville town marshal said a word, they simply turned away and began riding. When they had covered enough ground, they also turned westerly toward the mountains again, and Kennedy finally said, "Can you shoot that carbine one-handed?"

Bart had never done such a thing but was confident. He nevertheless had doubts about accuracy and said so. Jack Kennedy looked sardonically amused.

The drizzle had stopped, but the cloying mist closed down until visibility was limited to only a few yards ahead. Kennedy wagged his head about this entire undertaking but said nothing because whether he could see very far ahead or not, his voice would certainly carry.

Bart was letting the big bay horse pick his own way through the thickening mist. It was turning into a regular fog. The bay horse matched his gait to the pace of Kennedy's horse. The bay horse also stayed close.

Kennedy leaned once and whispered, "The only way we're going to find anyone in this mess is to ride right up onto them—and if that happens, I hope they haven't been listening to us coming."

Jack was wrong. There was another way they could find the outlaws. Somewhere in the middle distance to their right, which was northward, a horse whinnied. It could not have been Les Slater's animal because he could not have got down this far so soon.

Dimly through the shrouded atmosphere came the furious cursing of a man whose voice did not sound at all like that of Marshal Slater.

Bart and Kennedy dismounted, knelt with hobbles in hands to make sure their saddle animals would be here when they came back. Kennedy led the way, holding the borrowed Winchester across his body in both hands, leaning forward slightly and picking his feet up and putting them down very carefully—not so much to minimize noise as to avoid stumbling or falling.

Bart trailed Kennedy with a Winchester in his left hand. He was completely disoriented; he knew about where he was, maybe a half to three quarters of a mile east of the mountains, but that was all he knew.

He hoped very hard that they were west of the ambushers, but if this was so, he and Kennedy were not very far behind them. Otherwise, they would have been unable to hear that renegade curse his horse.

Kennedy stopped very abruptly and slowly sank to one knee. Bart saw nothing, but he followed his companion's example. The smell of woodsmoke was getting strong, but the actual fire appeared through the thick, settling fog as little more than a pinprick red glow ahead of Bart and a couple of degrees southward.

CHAPTER 18

The Showdown

A voice Bart recognized instantly, even muffled by distance and fog, suddenly said, "Well, where the hell are they?"

Walt!

Bart had spent a long evening with him and had had other conversations with the wiry old man who had claimed to be the liveryman up at Stillwater.

Kennedy probably did not recognize the voice, but he did not have to; his interest was in locating the bushwhackers, not in indentifying them. He turned his head, and Bart leaned to whisper. "That's the one who shot the cook. His name is Walt."

Kennedy nodded and faced forward. For a while he did not move. The plan had been to await the arrival of the U.S. deputy marshal. The longer Kennedy knelt without moving, the longer it seemed that he intended to wait.

Bart leaned on the borrowed Winchester, wishing he'd borrowed a six-gun instead. Even shooting with his left hand, he could at least manipulate a six-gun. Saddleguns required two hands.

The fog was beginning to rise, not far and not very rapidly, but visibility was improving at ground level.

Vaguely, Bart could make out rocks large enough to hide kneeling men. He did not remember seeing them before, but the only other time he had ridden through this area he had been a country mile southward, back down where the lava-rock caves were.

There were also trees, not many and not very thrifty ones, but adequate to shield ambushers. He and Jack Kennedy got down lower, because if they could see better, so could the outlaws.

There was shelter, but in order to reach it they would have to move, and movement of any kind was sure to attract attention from the invisible watchers behind the rocks.

Kennedy alternately looked toward the rocks and north-ward in the direction Slater would appear from. Bart saw a horse, than a second horse. They were hobbled and motionless. They were also head-hung tired. It occurred to him this could be the reason the outlaws had given up trying to reach the mountains before turning on their pursuers. They had ridden those animals hard all night, and even though they had stopped several times, the last time to wait out the downpour, horses could not withstand that kind of abuse indefinitely, even when they were rested and allowed to graze.

Kennedy leaned and whispered. "Watch those two pointy rocks with the gap between them on our left. There's someone over there."

He was correct. Bart saw the hunched back and shoulders of a man wearing a soggy hat whose brim drooped. The man moved into the gap between the conical rocks, then moved away from it. He was holding a Winchester in one hand, and he was looking in the direction of the firelight.

Bart assumed the other outlaws were also watching the fire, which was their bait for the men chasing them. He tapped Jack's arm and whispered to him. "Now that it's gettin' easier to see they'll spot Slater for sure when he rides toward their hiding places. They will blow him out of the saddle." Bart jutted his chin in the direction of the conical rocks. "I don't want to shoot that man in the back."

Marshal Kennedy considered the conical rocks without speaking or changing expression. He said, "Slater's not going to know they're hiding in those rocks. . . . Let's see if we can crawl a little closer, and if we can, I'll give them a chance to quit."

They crawled. The grass was wet, the muddy earth was cold, and Bart had trouble hitching along using only one arm, and that one with a Winchester in the hand. But evidently the outlaws were still facing in the opposite direction, toward their fire, because no one turned, saw them, and yelled a warning to the other outlaws.

Kennedy was within fifteen yards of the conical rocks when a man moved between them, his back to the crawling men, his body supported by the Winchester he had planted butt-down and was leaning on as he peered eastward where the rising fog revealed that the fire was beginning to burn down.

Jack shot Bart a look, then raised up very slowly out of the mud and grass, pushed his Winchester ahead, and waited for the outlaw to turn. But the man never did—he softly called to someone nearby that neither of the men behind him could see.

"Walt, they should have been out there by now."

The answer he got back was curt. "Naw, they got to scout around if they figure we're settin' over there drying out. They're going to reconnoiter. Give 'em a little more time."

The complaining man said, "Give 'em more time? Walt, we can make it into the mountains now. Them horses are strong enough for that. I'd feel a lot better if we was among them trees up there."

This time Walt's answer was delayed, and when he spoke again, his voice was almost a whisper. "Someone's coming from up north. Watch up there through the underbrush and trees. It's a rider, sure as hell."

Kennedy turned to stare at Bart, and the horse-breaker shoved up onto one knee using the Winchester as a crutch. They both stared northward. Bart did not see a horseman, but he was willing to believe the outlaws had because by now Les Slater had had enough time to get down this far. Bart nudged Kennedy and tilted his head toward the conical rocks.

Kennedy understood, raised his saddlegun, wiped mud off the butt-plate, and settled the weapon into the curve of his right shoulder. Then they waited until the man beyond the conical rocks appeared again. When he did, he was still looking in the opposite direction.

Kennedy spoke in a tone of voice only a notch or two above normal when he said, "Mister, let go of that carbine! Don't turn, and don't try to duck away—just let go of the Winchester!"

The startled outlaw did turn. He twisted violently from the waist to look back. Bart held his breath expecting Kennedy to shoot; instead the town marshal again called upon the startled outlaw to drop his weapon. The outlaw did not obey, and somewhere south of him a man's quick, alarmed voice called out. "What the hell is it? What's out there, Slim?"

Slim ignored the questions. He stared steadily at Kennedy and Bart for the better part of five seconds, then tightened his body and in a blur of speed, threw himself sideways as Kennedy fired. The bullet sent razor-sharp flakes of rock in all directions, but it did not appear that it had hit the outlaw.

But it had done something else, it had brought all the other outlaws around facing in the opposite direction from the fire.

Kennedy lunged ahead and landed belly-down at the base of the largest of the pair of conical rocks. He twisted to watch Bart struggling desperately to reach the same protection using only one arm to accomplish it.

A bullet came from among the big boulders and plowed gouts of mud behind Bart. That encouraged him to make an even greater effort to reach shelter. He made it and pushed as close to the other conical rock as he could, breathing hard and expecting Walt, or whoever it had been who fired at him, to stand up for a second try.

The initiative moved elsewhere as someone bawled like a bay steer and followed that with some rapid-fire handgun shooting. The answering gunfire came from beyond the rock field to the north, and whoever was out there fired systematically and without haste. Kennedy yelled across the little distance separating him from Bart. "Slater!"

The ambushers were no longer in a position to accomplish what they had built that fire for; they no longer had the advantage of surprise favoring them. But they still had the rock field to hide in, and that was almost as good as having their ambush prove successful.

Slater had emptied his handgun and was now flat down in the muddy tall grass with his carbine. Neither Bart nor Jack could see him, but as long as he systematically fired back at the alarmed outlaws who were trying to pinpoint his position, Bart and Jack Kennedy had time to shift position a little, get closer to the rounded sides of the conical rocks.

Kennedy raised his Winchester, took long aim, and fired. Someone farther in the field of big rocks squawked from a near-miss and turned to find Kennedy, but the town marshal had pulled back the moment he had fired, so there was nothing for the outlaw to aim at.

Bart, with his borrowed Winchester settled into a crack of rock, hunched around the gun, cocked it with his left hand, and waited for a target. It was a long wait. The outlaws had enemies on their left and behind them. They were being especially careful now that the first shock of discovering they had been flanked soaked in.

A man called out in a deep, strong voice, and Bart recognized the voice of Jess Morris—or Hugh Thompson.

But there was not even an arm or leg in sight. The outlaws were hugging rocks exactly as Bart and Jack Kennedy were doing.

Slater stopped firing. Bart thought he was probably reloading, but Bart was wrong: Slater was waiting, and when one of the outlaws moved, Slater fired. Bart saw one of the outlaws spring straight up, then twist half around as he crumpled, falling across a boulder facedown. His hat dropped, and the man did not move again.

Bart finally saw a head and a pair of shoulders come up as another outlaw stared at the man lying across the rock. He fired. The outlaw was punched hard by the impact of a bullet and rolled in the mud. He was almost completely in plain sight. Bart cocked the carbine and aimed again but did not fire because a voice he recognized as belonging to Walt suddenly yelled out.

"That's enough!"

Immediately a second hidden man answered. "Like hell!" Bart recognized that voice too, it belonged to Jess Morris. It was followed by a furious round of gunfire from a jumble of black rocks near the center of the field of rocks. Bart shifted his carbine and crouched over it with his left hand against the triggerguard, but when the bullet came that ended the fight, it arrived from the tall grass to the north. Slater had found a vulnerable place among those rocks where the outlaw leader was crouching and drove a bullet straight through it.

The only indication that he had scored a hit was when the outlaw's right arm came up violently and the carbine in his grip went sailing beyond the protective stones.

This time when Walt cried out, no one fired in the direction of his voice. He said, "I quit. That's enough. Who are you, out there?"

Walt got an answer that ignored his question. The U.S. deputy marshal called back, saying, "Stand up! Leave your guns on the ground and stand up!"

Walt bridled. "There's a couple guns behind me."

Slater repeated his order. "Stand up without your guns. No one is going to shoot you."

Walt did not arise, but another outlaw did, with both arms over his head. He was facing north. Seconds passed before Slater called to Walt again. "Now you! On your feet!"

The wiry, old man came up very reluctantly. He did not look north, he looked west where Bart's carbine barrel was visible through the rocks.

For a short while there was not a sound, then Jack Kennedy arose and leaned across his conical stone, aiming at Walt with his Winchester. Bart thought Walt was going to jump away and drop behind the rocks. He crouched and seemed not to be breathing, but when Kennedy did not fire, Walt lost some of his tight-wound look.

Slater came up slowly and stiffly from the muddy grass, carbine held low in both hands. He walked to the edge of the rocks and halted. "Mr. Kennedy, make certain those two don't have guns," he said, and Jack leaned aside the Winchester, palmed his six-gun, and made his way through the jumble of rocks to Walt's side.

Bart stood up and lifted his saddlegun to the top of his rock and watched.

Marshal Slater picked his way among the big rocks to the place where he had fired his last shot. He stood a long time looking at something the other men could not see on the ground behind boulders, then he went in closer and leaned to pick up a six-gun and a carbine.

Kennedy moved from Walt to the other surviving outlaw, the man called Slim, who had originally been upon the far side of the pair of conical rocks. Kennedy roughly searched him, too, then stepped back and waited for Slater to join him.

Finally Bart left his Winchester against a rock and went into the field of boulders to join the two lawmen. He stepped past a short distance to crane down into the protected place where Slater had stopped first.

The burly man Bart had known as Jess Morris was lying on his back with both arms outflung. Slater's bullet had caught him through the body high up. He must have died almost instantly.

Bart stepped closer and knelt to rummage inside the dead man's shirt until he found the waterproof packet John Holbrook had given him with eleven thousand dollars in it. He also removed the deputy shiriff's badge before he returned to the area where Jack Kennedy and the federal officer were dragging the other dead outlaw off the rock he had fallen across.

Walt and the lanky outlaw called Slim watched woodenly as their dead companions were taken beyond the boulder field. They trailed the bodies out there, too, and when the federal officer was drying his hands on a blue bandanna, Walt said, "He thought it would be you, Slater. He told us when we busted out of Holbrook's yard that he probably should have shot you because otherwise when you got loose you'd still be after us."

The gray-eyed deputy U.S. marshal pocketed the bandanna while regarding his two captives. He turned away from them without a word to go after his carbine. Walt faced Bart and wagged his head. "You sure used us, cowboy. I believed you myself, even when I knew better."

Kennedy was reloading his handgun and ignored them all until Slater returned; then the pair of them left the prisoners in Bart's care and went after the saddle stock. The sky was darkening again, and it was a long ride back to the Holbrook place.

CHAPTER 19

Tired Horses, Tired Men

It did not rain again, but the overcast sky made the day appear to be ending when, in fact, it was actually only late afternoon as the party of horsemen turned eastward from the rock field. Kennedy and Slater led the two horses with corpses lashed belly-down across their saddles. Bart rode in the rear with Walt and the tall, skinny outlaw called Slim. He had Walt's six-gun shoved into his waistband. The muddy carbine was slung by its saddle-ring on the right side of his saddle.

The outlaws' horses seemed indifferent about the direction they were going in. They were badly used up and walked with no spring in their legs.

Bart had given the badge from the murdered Wyoming deputy to Les Slater. Slater also had the guns of the dead men tied to his saddle. Two miles along he did something he had not done before in Bart's sight: He fished for a plug of chewing tobacco and got a cud of it settled into his right cheek. Walt watched this with hungry eyes and asked if the U.S. marshal could spare some.

Slater turned to regard the old man for a long time and when Bart was sure he was going to refuse, Slater reined over and handed the plug to the outlaw. He retrieved it after Walt had got his chew, and rode ahead again, all without saying a word.

In fact, he was silent until they were halfway back toward Bart's yard, then he turned toward Walt and said, "Why didn't Thompson just take the eleven thousand after Holbrook gave it to him, and ride out?"

Walt expectorated before replying. "That was my idea, but he said sure as hell that old cowman had a cache somewhere, maybe in the house. He said them outlying cow outfits always keep a wad of cash on hand. He didn't want to leave until he got that too." Walt shook his head. "Hell, all the old man had in his safe was a couple of thousand dollars. That damned fool got us run down and captured for two thousand dollars. We could have got more'n that from a stagecoach with a bullion box on it."

Slater continued to eye the wiry older man. "When that Stillwater deputy rode into your camp—"

"How do you know he done that?" Walt interrupted to ask.

"Because I've been tracking people like Thompson and you most of my life. When he rode in, did he tell you who he was and why he was in the mountains?"

"Yeah. He told us a lot more too; he even told us what Mailer looked like and that there'd be a reward on him up in Wyoming. He set around the campfire with us drinking whiskey and coffee, talking his head off. Hugh kept pouring whiskey into his cup, and when the deputy finally crawled into his blankets, Hugh told us what he'd been thinking about—taking up Mailer's trail, the four of us, and getting that eleven thousand dollars. Then he shot the deputy and rolled him down a canyon."

Bart listened to all this with considerable interest. Hugh Thompson had been more than shrewd, he had also been imaginative. He had completely fooled Bart and John Holbrook. Bart had not begun to have vague doubts until a

day or two ago. Even then, it never occurred to him that
Thompson was not a deputy sheriff named Jess Morris from
Wyoming, as he had claimed.

Thompson had also been a very good actor. He'd had
answers for every question Bart and John Holbrook had
asked him. Bart shook his head. What had destroyed
Thompson had been greed; as Walt had said, if he had not
waited for a chance to rob John Holbrook, he could have
gotten away before Les Slater arrived from Holtville.

Kennedy had a question for Walt. He wanted the full
names of Walt, Slim, and the other man, the outlaw
Kennedy had killed back in the rock field.

Walt named each man, including himself. Then he lapsed
into silence and slouched along with his cud of chewing
tobacco to keep him company. He and the other captive did
not even look at each other, let alone engage in conversation. Bart's impression from this was that there was not a
whole lot of love lost between the younger outlaw and Walt.

By the time they reached Bart's yard, the day was truly
ending. Ordinarily Bart would have suggested that they lie
over until morning before riding on over to the Holbrook
place, even though the distance was not great, only three or
four miles. Not only were all the men hungry and tired, but
so were the horses. Nevertheless, Bart suggested to Kennedy and Slater that they continue eastward. Kennedy
looked unhappy at this prospect, but the federal officer was
agreeable.

It did not occur to Walt that Marshal Slater might have his
own reason for wishing to get back to the Holbrook place.

Bart reined away from his yard, and the bay horse
seemed about to balk. He knew where he was, and he
apparently was anxious to be home because usually when he
reached the yard he was unsaddled, turned into his corral,
and fed.

Jack Kennedy eyed his actions sourly. "Barn sour," he

said. "It don't take them long to learn where the haystack is." Kennedy had never liked the big bay horse.

Bart jockeyed him, kept him moving, and because Slater knew the solution to this situation and rode on ahead, when Bart put the mustang's head close to the rear end of Slater's horse, the impending challenge from the bay horse ended. He plodded out of the yard with all the other animals following along.

They were within sight of lamplight before Slater addressed Bart, giving him his first clue as to why the federal officer had not wanted to lie over at the Templeton place.

"Mailer wasn't with them, which means he was probably at the Holbrook place when we left."

Jack Kennedy was smoking a cigarette and eyed the federal officer askance. "You want him?" he asked.

Slater rode with his face toward the distant little pinpricks of light. "I want to talk to him," he said, being noncommittal.

Bart picked up where Kennedy had left off. "What about? The robbery up at Stillwater?"

Slater nodded, spat amber, and rode the balance of the way to the yard in silence.

Perhaps because they entered the yard from the west, and it was dark, no one came down to the barn when they took the horses inside to be off-saddled. But about the time they were standing in the front doorway with their prisoners, the range-boss appeared. He had come to the bunkhouse after they had ridden in and had heard them.

He eyed Slim and Walt, then raised his eyes to the federal officer. "That's all you got?"

Slater jerked his head. "No, we got Thompson and another one. We laid them out in the barn and used a wagon-canvas to cover them with. Where is Frank Mailer?"

Charley delayed his answer until he and Bart had exchanged a glance, and Bart almost imperceptibly nodded his head. "At the main house. . . . You fellows hungry?"

They were. Charley took them over to the cookshack, where a lamp was burning. The cook had a bandage on his head as large as a turban, but he looked around at them with clear eyes and a tough smile when he recognized their prisoners. He gestured with a large wooden spoon. "Set, boys. The coffee's still hot, and I can rassle up leftovers in a few minutes." He regarded Walt for a moment, then said, "You're the one who shot me."

Walt stood still, watching the large man with the paunch.

The cook muttered something and turned toward the stove. "Set with the rest of 'em, you bastard," he said.

Charley left them and headed for the main house. Slater watched him go, but said nothing. Their coffee arrived and it was hot. By lamplight they could look at one another and see how filthy, soggy, and disreputable they looked. Jack Kennedy grinned, something he did not do often. "Bart, you look like hell. How is your arm?"

It ached. "Passable, Jack, passable."

The cook brought bowls of beef stew that was aromatic and steaming. He fed the man who had shot him last. After Walt had taken a mouthful of stew the cook leaned toward him and said, "Didn't you see me put that wolf poison in it?"

Walt raised a startled pair of eyes. The cook laughed, and everyone joined in, except Walt. He looked at the bowl in front of him and put down the spoon as the others continued eating. From over in front of his big iron cook-stove the cook said, "Naw. I just wanted to see you worry a little. You can eat it. I've never poisoned anything in my life."

All five men ate with gusto. They had been ravenous before reaching the Holbrook yard and after smelling food nothing, not even wild horses, could have distracted them from their meal. The tall, lean outlaw called Slim ate three bowlfuls and complimented the cook on the way he seasoned beef stew. The cook was pleased and showed it. It was not common on working cow outfits for anyone to say anything good about the food. Complimenting *cocineros* was said to make them even more cantankerous than they ordinarily were.

Charley Lord and another rangeman walked in and leaned on both sides of the door, looking stonily at the two prisoners. They said nothing, and no one spoke to them until all the bowls and coffee cups had been emptied at least twice; then Les Slater boldly eyed the pair of motionless Holbrook men.

"I'd be obliged," he told them, "if you gents would chain these two renegades in out of the rain tonight."

Charley, with arms crossed over his chest, nodded at Slater and said, "In the barn." He regarded the federal officer for a moment, then swung his attention to Jack Kennedy. "They'd like to talk to you gents over at the main house."

Bart straightened on his bench. He wanted to ask if the surgery had been performed, but restrained himself until they stepped outside and he drew the range-boss aside.

"Did Mailer work on Mr. Holbrook this morning?" Bart asked.

Charley woodenly nodded. "Yeah. Early. Not more'n a half hour after you fellows left the yard."

"How is he, Charley?"

"I haven't been allowed in to see him, but Nan said this afternoon that he was coming out from under whatever the doctor gave him to make him unconscious."

"Didn't she say how he was?"

"No. Just that he was in bed knocked out."

Bart approached the subject from a different angle. "How about Frank Mailer; what's he got to say?"

Charley sighed. "As far as I know, nothing, but he hasn't come out of the house all day. Nan only came out for a few minutes because she knew the riders were worried." Charley cocked his head, listening to men rising from the long table inside. "What happened to that phony Wyoming deputy?"

"Marshal Slater shot him in some rocks about a day's ride west over beyond my range. Jack Kennedy got the other one that's over in the barn under that wagon-canvas."

Charley was turning toward the door at the sound of booted men approaching it from inside as he said, "Those lawmen want Dr. Mailer?"

Bart did not have a good answer, so it was just as well that Kennedy and Slater were approaching.

The prisoners emerged from the cookshack, followed by a rangeman and the cook, but he only came as far as the door, then turned back.

Charley and the rangeman closed in around Walt and Slim and herded them off in the direction of the barn. There was a lantern hanging inside over there, and two more rangemen were slouching in the front barn opening.

Marshal Slater watched as his prisoners were surrounded by John Holbrook's riders and taken deeper into the barn; then he turned and smiled at Jack Kennedy. "They're fed, and they'll sleep like dead men. Mr. Kennedy, you got a cell for them over at Holtville?"

Jack nodded. He was rolling a smoke and was not paying attention to anything else. "Yeah. I got six cages. Since I been town marshal I've never had all six full at once." He lipped the cigarette, raked a match across the seat of his britches, lighted up, and blew smoke into the heavy, damp night air.

Charley came out of the barn and sauntered back toward the waiting men up there. "You gents want to wash up before you go to the main house? You look like you been wallowing in a mud sump with the pigs."

He took them to the wash-rack out behind the bunkhouse, provided them with a thick bar of brown soap and what passed for towels, which were actually flour sacks that had been emptied and boiled before being assigned their present role.

While the three men scrubbed and made themselves as presentable as they could, Charley listened to details of their pursuit and their meeting with the outlaws.

They told him the story from the time they had left the Holbrook yard until they had returned to it.

Charley left them briefly to make sure the men in the barn had done their work well, then returned as they were standing out front on the bunkhouse porch, and escorted them over to the main house.

There was not a star in sight. It was finally beginning to rain again. It was so dark by now that it was impossible to determine where the ground ended and the sky began.

CHAPTER 20

Nan Holbrook's Longest Day

When Nan Holbrook admitted Bart and the two lawmen to the main house, she looked drawn and tired. The parlor smelled like a hospital. A lighted lamp on a large oak table seemed to be the only light in the house; the distant hallway was dark, as was the kitchen.

Nan motioned for the three visitors to be seated and waited until the range-boss had gone back outside before speaking.

She asked about the outlaws, and Marshal Slater told her what had happened, though Bart thought Nan already knew; he was sure that the range-boss had told her when he had left the cookshack while the lawmen, Bart, and their prisoners were eating.

She offered them coffee, and they declined. She stood for a moment, as though undecided, before saying, "You knew my father was to have surgery this morning." When all three men sat stoically watching her face, she also said, "The arrowhead was removed. My father was unconscious until this afternoon; when he began coming around he was like someone in a daze. He is still pretty much that way, but

154

if you'd care to see him, I'll take you as far as the bedroom door. But I don't think you should talk to him—you will have to wait until tomorrow to talk to him."

Jack Kennedy extended his legs and crossed them at the ankles. He looked from Slater to Bart, then up at Nan Holbrook, evidently to see if the other two men were going to speak. When they did not, Kennedy asked a question. "Did it work; was the surgery successful?"

Nan eyed Marshal Kennedy for a moment and said, "I don't know. No one will know until he is fully conscious. . . . It required an hour to perform the surgery. It seemed to me to have been done in a very efficient and professional manner." .

Les Slater considered the pictures on the distant mantel briefly before putting his attention upon Nan. He said, "You haven't mentioned the surgeon."

She looked squarely at the federal officer. "He was Dr. Frank Mailer."

Slater nodded his head. "And where is Dr. Mailer now?"

"Sleeping. It was very hard on him."

Nan shook her head. "Not tonight, Mr. Slater. Tomorrow."

The pale-eyed, tall federal officer rose from his chair. When he spoke, he surprised Bart, who would not have thought the taciturn U.S. marshal was a man of tact. Slater said, "Miss Holbrook, we have two outlaws chained down in your barn. The doctor is a fugitive from the law. I appreciate your feelings about him, but my job requires that fugitives, whether they're federal or state fugitives, be put under restraint. Even sleeping ones who are exhausted after having done surgery. . . . I don't have to talk to Dr. Mailer tonight—that can wait—but I do want to be absolutely certain he will be here for me to talk to in the morning."

Nan moved toward a massive, old hand-carved sideboard

as she replied to the federal marshal. "Do you mean chains, Mr. Slater?"

The answer she was given was a blunt "Yes."

Nan leaned against the sideboard, looking directly at the federal lawman, black eyes unwavering. "I don't think so," she told him. "Not in this house where we have reason to feel beholden to Dr. Mailer. Anyway, he's not going to sneak away in the night."

Slater's brows raised a little. "You know that for a fact, ma'am?"

"Yes. He told my father early this morning that he was not going to run one more step, that when you and Mr. Kennedy returned, he would be here waiting."

Slater did not say anything.

"Marshal," Jack Kennedy said to Slater, "we're dog-tired. If he isn't here come morning I'll personally guarantee you to run him down and fetch him back." Kennedy also rose from his chair. "Now let's go get some rest. As far as I'm concerned, this talk is finished." Kennedy started for the door. As he passed Bart, he motioned to him. Bart followed him to the door, where Kennedy turned, big and unyielding. "Good night," he said to Nan, then looked stonily at Les Slater. "Marshal, you want me to carry you down to the bunkhouse?"

Not a person in the parlor doubted but that Jack Kennedy would do exactly that, and not even Les Slater seemed to doubt that the big, powerfully muscled-up town marshal could do it. He shook his head and started for the door. When he reached it, Nan said, "He will be here, Mr. Slater. Don't you doubt it. Good night."

When they were outside on the porch, Slater glared at Jack Kennedy. "Marshal, for all we know he's already fifteen miles away and still riding."

Kennedy was building a cigarette and did not look up from it when he softly said, "Mr. Slater, I don't take it kindly you calling that lady in there a liar." Jack lipped his smoke but made no attempt to light it as he stared coldly at the federal lawman.

Slater sighed in frustration. He had only wanted to see Frank Mailer, not talk to him. He simply wanted to see with his own eyes that Mailer was indeed in the house. With a fierce grunt he walked down off the porch in the direction of the bunkhouse. Jack Kennedy started to follow, then turned, and winked owlishly at Bart. Kennedy had taken the initiative in the parlor and had kept it out on the veranda. He was satisfied; it was not every day a cow-town lawman could take a federal deputy marshal down a peg.

Before Bart reached the bottom step a soft voice from up on the porch in the darkness said, "Bart, can I see you for a minute?"

All three men halted, Slater and Kennedy looking back at the soft outline of the handsome woman up there under the wooden overhang. Then Kennedy grunted, reached to give Les Slater a little shove, and kept walking, driving the federal officer ahead of him all the way down to the lighted bunkhouse through a soft rain.

Bart returned to the porch. Nan motioned toward a chair and sat down on an adjoining one. She pushed out a very tired smile. "You were right; it was terrible. I didn't faint, but I think I would have if Dr. Mailer hadn't made me drink some watered whiskey."

Bart got comfortable and watched the pair of lawmen disappear into the bunkhouse door. Then he looked around and asked quietly, "Was it a success, Nan?"

"We don't know. I told you in the house—we won't know until my father is fully conscious again. I suppose Dad will know before the rest of us do; he was coming around this afternoon and sometime during the night he will be back to normal." She turned toward him. "If he can move a leg or wiggle a toe, Dr. Mailer said it will have been a success."

Bart was silent a long time. The waiting was clearly tearing Nan part. He tried to be supportive by saying, "He'll be all right."

She sounded faintly despairing. "Bart, you weren't there. Dr. Mailer had a terrible time freeing the arrowpoint. Bone had grown around it. I had to mop sweat off the doctor's face every couple of minutes."

"He got it out intact?"

She nodded. "It left an opening in one of the back bones."

"Will that heal closed?"

"Dr. Mailer said it will, but it will take a long time. And in the meanwhile my father has to be very careful not to do anything that might further weaken the bone. Until it heals, any damage—getting bucked off a horse, for instance— could cripple him for life, could leave him with no feeling in his legs."

"He's not going to ride a bucking horse, Nan."

She looked fiercely at him. "He's not going to ride *any* horse, Bart. He's not even going to drive his buggy for six months." She let a moment of silence pass, then sank back in her chair and looked down through the drizzling rainfall in the direction of the lighted bunkhouse. "That man is not going to take Dr. Mailer out of this yard!" Her profile was set in an ironlike cast. "Even it it turns out that my father can't use his legs, Bart, he won't have that constant pain anymore. Dr. Mailer did his best, and to me, he seemed very skilled at his work. I know he helped my father; maybe not as much as my father wanted to be helped—we won't know about that until morning—but he certainly helped him just by removing the arrowhead. . . . Bart, no one is going to put Frank Mailer in chains and take him out of this yard. Not Marshal Kennedy, not Marshal Slater, not the entire U.S. army!"

She suddenly turned toward him again, her expression

softening in the shadows. "I'm sorry. That's the second time I only thought about my problems and not yours. How is the arm?"

He smiled at her. "It aches a little, maybe because I had to wallow around in the mud with it, and maybe because of the wet weather, but it's all right."

She leaned to see him better in the semidarkness, then stood up. "No, it is not all right. You come out to the kitchen with me. I can smell that bandage from here."

He started to protest but arose and followed her through the house to the kitchen. Bart sat at the table out there while she went after fresh, clean bandaging material. It was warm, fragrant, and comfortable in the kitchen. By the time Nan returned he had fallen asleep.

She stood looking at him for a moment, then bent to kiss his stubbly cheek before turning brisk as she awakened him and went to work cutting away the filthy bandage.

Beneath it his flesh was white and wrinkled from being soaked. She dried the arm very carefully and wrapped it in a new bandage. As she was tying it, she looked up at him. "All right? Not too tight?"

He smiled. "Just right. You'd make a good nurse."

She regarded the bandaged arm and was satisfied. Then she started to tell him to put it back inside the front of his shirt, and suddenly rose to leave the room. She returned with a clean shirt from her father's dresser drawer.

She helped him into the clean shirt. It fit. She buttoned it for him and turned away while he got the shirttail stuffed into his britches using his left hand. When she turned back, she smiled. "Now what you need is a shave."

He shook his head slowly. "I'll take care of that when I get home," he told her.

"You're going to spend the night here, Bart."

He was perfectly willing to stay. Both he and the bay horse'd had enough for one day, but when she mentioned a spare bedroom in the house, he said, "The bunkhouse will do just fine. By the way, how are the emigrants?"

"Fine. The baby slept most of the day. Emily was a great help around the house today. She cooked for all of us while Dr. Mailer and I were busy. Her husband split enough kindling in the woodshed to last a month." Nan paused, regarding him pensively before adding a little more. "I'm going to ask my father if he'll give them a hundred acres up near the foothills where they had their wagon-camp. We don't need it, and it's good deep ground."

Bart's eyes crinkled slowly. "Do you think he'll do it? I've heard your pa talk about settlers."

She had doubts, too, but could be just as determined as her father. "They'll be out of sight from here. They'll even be a long day's ride from the yard. And we've always had trouble with varmints coming out of the mountains up there to kill livestock. Mr. Wilton could kill wolves and panthers. That ought to be worth something. And one hundred acres near the mountains doesn't mean a thing to us. We already own more land than we have livestock to keep the grass down."

He picked up his soggy hat and said good night. He went through the parlor to the front door, and she followed him out to the porch. He dropped on the old hat as she said, "Let me know what your pa says about giving away that land" and started down off the porch. She called him just as he reached the ground.

"Bart, will you come around to the kitchen first thing in the morning?"

He nodded. "Sure. Be glad to."

She was clasping her hands. "I . . . I'm going to need someone to hold my hand. Tomorrow morning may very well be the most important day of my life."

He understood. "And of your pa's life too. Good night."

She remained on the porch until he disappeared into the darkened bunkhouse, then went slowly back indoors. She could not remember ever having felt as tired and anxious as she felt tonight.

Before going to her room she went to stand in the doorway of her father's bedroom, where wet starshine shone upon the seemingly lifeless, deeply breathing man sleeping on his stomach.

She stood a long time saying a fervent prayer, then finally went off to her own bedroom. It was a little past midnight.

CHAPTER 21

The Moving Storm

Slater's bunk was empty when Bart awakened and rolled out to pull on his boots. Jack Kennedy was snoring across the room making noises like a pig caught under a gate.

The range-riders were stirring, and when Bart got outside in the chilly damp predawn, there was a light over at the cookshack. There was also one in the kitchen of the main house, but there was no sign of the deputy U.S. marshal, so Bart went down to the barn to pitch feed to the horses. There he finally encountered Les Slater leaning on a corral watching the horses. When Bart appeared, Slater jutted his jaw upward. There were no clouds, and the stars were beginning to fade. Slater said, "Today'll be the big day for the Holbrooks, eh?"

Bart nodded, stepped closer, and looked for his bay horse. The animal looked back at him from among a half dozen other horses.

Bart said, "I came down to pitch feed, but you got two good arms, and I only have one. Would you mind?"

They returned to the barn for a pitchfork and for as long as was required to tote hay to corrals and pitch it over, the lawman said nothing. But when he had finished and was leaning on the fork watching the horses eat, he said, "Kennedy snores like a buffalo. Is he married?"

"Yes."

Slater looked amused as he wagged his head. Then he jerked his head in the direction of the main house. "I was going to go over there."

That had also been the horse-breaker's intention, but he was not sure Nan would welcome him arriving with the federal lawman so he said, "There'll be grub and hot coffee at the cookshack. If you're still worrying about Mailer . . ."

Slater eyed the younger man. "You figure it'd be better if I let the folks at the main house get set for the day before I showed up, eh?"

Bart nodded. "Something like that."

They continued to stand beside the corral for another minute or so before Marshal Slater turned and gave Bart a light slap on the shoulder. "All right. See you directly." He walked past Bart toward the cookshack."

Bart waited until the lawman was inside before he headed for the side of the main house. When he knocked, Nan opened the kitchen door for him. She had coffee heating, and her face was flushed because the kitchen was hot. She looked past before closing the door and turned to say, "The storm is past?"

He nodded and waited for her to fill a cup with coffee for him, then told her of meeting Slater behind the barn. She looked worried as she filled a second cup for herself. As she was tasting it and eyeing Bart over the rim, a man's heavy footsteps sounded from the parlor.

Frank Mailer appeared in the doorway. He had scrubbed but had not shaved, so he had salt-and-pepper stubble. Nan handed him a cup of coffee, which he took to the table where he sat down regarding the cup for a moment before raising his eyes to her face.

"Is he awake?" he asked.

She had not looked in on her father. "I don't know."

Mailer raised his cup. "Drink it down," he told them, "and we'll go see. No point in prolonging this."

Bart finished half his cupful and put the cup aside. Nan did not even drink that much before setting her cup on the table. Frank Mailer drank slowly and stared steadily at the door. Bart thought the older man looked more resigned than worried, which was perhaps about the way he felt. A man could only do his utmost; beyond that in a situation of this kind the outcome rested upon things over which he could exert no control.

The sky was brightening from black to gunmetal-gray, the stars were winking out a few dozen at a time, and finally now there was a light down at the bunkhouse as Dr. Mailer picked up the lamp and led the way through the parlor to the hallway and into John Holbrook's bedroom. He walked over to a small table and placed the lamp upon it, then turned.

The room was alight. All three of them looked at the man in the bed. John Holbrook looked straight back at them and, because his face was expressionless, Bart's heart sank. No one spoke until Frank Mailer stepped to the end of the bed and tossed the blankets aside to expose Holbrook's legs and feet. He said "Move your toes" in a rough tone of voice.

Bart was scarcely breathing. He felt Nan's fingers steal into his left hand. He held them tightly. Her black eyes were wide, her face pale.

Nothing happened.

Mailer stepped around to the side of the bed where he and Holbrook could see each other and repeated his earlier order. "Move your toes, John."

Holbrook spoke in a perfectly clear, calm tone of voice. "They'll move, Frank. Watch."

Mailer stepped back near the lower end of the bed and leaned slightly. Bart and Nan were also watching. Her father moved his toes, not vigorously, but he moved them.

Frank Mailer straightened up, letting his breath out in a long sigh. He said, "Did you try it before?"

Holbrook answered in the same steady tone of voice. "Yes. Some time after midnight, when I awakened with the haziness gone from my mind."

Mailer went to a chair and sank down upon it. Nan freed her fingers and went forward to kiss her father. She was crying without making a sound. Bart approached the bed and smiled. Old Holbrook smiled back and said, "You look like hell."

Bart nodded.

Holbrook looked him up and down, then said, "Where did you get that shirt?"

Bart's smile deepened. "You like it? Fits pretty well, doesn't it? It's your shirt, but I think I'll keep it."

Holbrook's eyes brightened with humor. "All right. Anything else I got you want?"

Bart laughed and looked at Nan, who blushed a little.

Holbrook shifted his gaze to the man on the chair. "Frank, by gawd, I owe you."

Mailer ignored that. "Does your back hurt, John?"

"Hell yes, it hurts."

"I'll get you some laudanum."

"No. I've had pain in my back for about as many years as you are old. But this time, it's a different kind of pain. It'll let up in time . . . Frank?"

"John?"

"I'll be able to walk."

"Yes. But not right away. You'll have to stay in bed for a while, then start out slow and easy, but yes, you'll be able to walk. As for the pain—give it six months for the vertebrae to heal closed. After that you should be fine. We'll talk about this later. You need rest and lots of it. Are you hungry?"

"No. Frank, I've been lying here most of the night thinking. Do you still have that eleven thousand dollars?"

"Yes. I hid it in the cellar."

"Keep it."

"I can't keep it, John. There are two lawmen down in your bunkhouse waiting to take it and me back."

"No. You keep it. I gave that phony Deputy Morris eleven thousand from my safe and let him think it was the money you got from the Stillwater bank."

Bart said to Holbrook, "The federal marshal, Jack Kennedy, and I caught up with Hugh Thompson and his partners west of here yesterday. There was a fight. Slater killed Morris. Slater has the money now along with the deputy sheriff's badge. When you're up to it, John, I'll tell you about it."

Holbrook said, "You come around here where I can see you. You, too, Nan." When they had obeyed, Holbrook looked at them with a hard glint in his eyes. "Jack Kennedy's a reasonable man. I've known him ever since he arrived in Blue Basin. He's not going to make trouble. Bart, you tell that deputy U.S. lawman to take that eleven thousand dollars back up north and give it to the sheriff up there. You tell him if he tries to take Frank Mailer out of this yard, I'll plant him out yonder in the ranch graveyard."

A soft, steely voice spoke from just beyond the bedroom doorway as Marshal Slater moved forward out of the darkened hallway into the light of the bedroom. "Glad to know you're all right, Mr. Holbrook. I guess you are, or you wouldn't be talking like that."

Slater approached the bed. "The kitchen door was open, so I came in." He gazed steadily at the man in the bed, and eventually swung his attention to the man on the chair. "You're Frank Mailer?"

The doctor nodded. "Yes."

"Will he walk again?" Slater asked.

Frank repeated the word. "Yes." Then he leaned to arise from the chair as he said, "We can talk outside, Marshal. Mr. Holbrook needs quiet and rest and no excitement."

Slater put a slow look at the other people in the room and gently inclined his head. He would have stepped clear of the door, but John Holbrook spoke and stopped him in his tracks. "He's not going out of this yard with you, Marshal."

Slater met old Holbrook's menacing gaze without flinching. "I haven't said that he was, Mr. Holbrook, but I'd like to talk to him."

Holbrook said, "Go with them, Bart. If he tries to get Frank on a horse, you tell Charley and the other riders to bring him back in here to me with his arms tied behind his back!"

Slater raised an eyebrow at the unarmed and one-armed horse-breaker, then nodded for Bart and Frank Mailer to precede him out of the room.

When they were gone, Holbrook looked at his daughter. She was dry-eyed now, her expression remained the same, deeply etched with heartfelt gratitude and relief from the agony and uncertainty she had had to live with since early yesterday morning. He said, "I thanked God a lot last night, Nan. I even asked Him to let your mother know I finally got that thing out of my back because it used to worry her sick." He was silent for a moment and did not take his eyes off her face. "I know you were worried."

She nodded without trusting herself to speak. The tears were back, unshed and hot.

"Not altogether about me, Nan. About the horse-breaker, too, when he went after that renegade deputy sheriff. . . . Nan, I can't lose you. Especially not now when you're going to have to be my legs as well as my eyes until I can get around by myself."

She said, "Lose me?"

"To Bart Templeton, honey."

They looked at each other for a long time before he spoke again. "Back pain don't make a man blind. You and Bart . . . The way he looks at you and the way you look at him." Holbrook's eyes clouded slightly. "I know. I went through the exact same thing with your mother. She was like you—straight as an arrow with eyes that pulled a man's heartstrings . . . He's a good man, Nan. Resourceful, tough, and without any pretense. But I'm going to be flat on my back for a long time . . ."

She ran the back of one hand across her eyes quickly and leaned to kiss him again. "I'll be here for as long as you need me. Now get some rest."

As she reached the doorway, he called to her. "Nan, go tell Charley those lawmen aren't to take Frank out of the yard . . . and ask Jack Kennedy to come see me, please."

She nodded and went back to the kitchen to stoke the fire beneath the coffeepot before going out into the yard to find the range-boss and the Holtville town marshal.

Until she left the house she had no idea what a magnificent day this was turning into. The earth was drying, the sun was high, the sky was a flawless azure color.

CHAPTER 22

Men and Principles

Where Marshal Slater and Frank Mailer were leaning on the tie rack with Bart down in front of the barn, Bart saw Nan come out of the house and meet Charley Lord over near the shoeing shed. He watched the earnest way she spoke to him, and when Charley turned to look in the direction of the men at the tie rack in front of the barn, Bart thought he knew what Nan told him.

He watched her walk back to the main house. Still had his eyes on her when the deputy federal marshal told Frank Mailer he had the bank loot inside his shirt.

Mailer replied, "No, that's Mr. Holbrook's money, Marshal" and explained why Holbrook had said it was the bank loot.

Slater flicked a questioning look at Bart, who nodded his head in verification, then Slater said, "Where is the bank money, Doctor?"

"Hidden over at the main house. I'll get it for you."

"I'd say Holbrook thinks a lot of ¸ou to do something like that. Eleven thousand dollars is a lot of money. More than most men could save in a lifetime."

Frank leaned, continued to look at the ground, and said nothing.

"I'm in a kind of peculiar situation, Doctor. I'm a lawman. My job is to apprehand fugitives. On the other hand, we don't stick our noses into regional troubles unless a federal law has been violated. Still and all, bank robbery isn't something a man can turn his back on. You understand?"

Mailer disconsolately inclined his head and still did not meet the unwavering pale-gray eyes of the lawman.

"That would be more in Mr. Kennedy's area to take you in and lock you up until Wyoming lawmen can come down and get you with an extradition warrant." Slater leaned on the tie-pole for a moment in silence, then finally said, "I'll tell you gents something: I've been at my trade over twenty years and in that length of time I've run down my share of renegades, and I've heard every darned excuse men can think up about why what outlaws did was not a crime. . . . I'll be damned if I ever ran into anyone like you before.

"They tell us never to get involved, to stay aloof, not to make judgements about guilt or innocence; that's for the courts to do." Slater squinted into the distance. "I never had a bit of trouble obeying those rules until now.

"The emigrant lady would have bled to death, her baby would most likely have died, too, and that would have likely ruined the life of the emigrant man. You saved three lives, Doctor; that's worth something—especially to me. I was married once, years ago. My wife died in childbirth. There wasn't a darned thing I could do, and the doctor was a cow-town veterinarian. There wasn't anyone else. . . . I can tell you even now, many years later, what that emigrant man would have gone through. A memory like that never stops haunting."

Bart and Frank were regarding the tall, gray-eyed man.

When he stopped speaking and dug out a plug to gnaw a corner off, they did not move or speak.

Slater continued, "Doctor, I didn't get you down here to preach to you . . . I guess what I really had to do was sort it all out in my mind; balance my personal judgment against the rules I've been living by for twenty years."

Slater spat, moved around on the rack, and looked straight at Frank Mailer. 'I got a question for you: That work you did on Holbrook—it wasn't something just any doctor could do, was it?"

"Well, not *any* doctor, Marshal. A doctor would also have to be a surgeon."

Slater spat again and brushed Frank's remark aside. "And you took a hell of a risk, didn't you?"

Frank studied his hands for a moment before slowly nodding his head without saying much. "Yes. A risk for me and a worse risk for John Holbrook."

"Doctor, how close could a man come to saying what you did amounted to a miracle?"

Frank straightened up off the rack looking embarrassed. "Not a miracle. A little skill and a lot of luck, but not a miracle."

Slater said, "The law is the law. It was made by men, and therefore it's not always perfect, or even very wise. . . . I'll be damned if I'm going to take a narrow view of what I've witnessed down here. Anyway, I'll see that they get their money back up in Wyoming. Beyond that, I doubt very much that they'll do anything. I especially don't think the banker will because I'm going to have a long talk with him." Slater's hard, direct eyes showed a faint hint of cold humor when he looked around again. "I can be pretty persuasive, gents, especially with someone who founded his bank on stolen money to begin with."

Bart said, "What about Denver; the U.S. Marshal up there?"

Slater shrugged. "What about him? He's been wanting

Hugh Thompson's scalp for a long time. I'll give him the next best thing: Thompson's guns and wallet, saddle, everything else to prove Thompson is dead. And I'll give him Walt and Slim to verify that I killed Thompson. That's all he wants. Walt and Slim won't know anything about Mailer being left behind and wouldn't care much about him, if they did. Mailer's not going to be on a federal list of fugitives for anything; he didn't break a federal law."

Mailer spoke to Slater. "You're taking a big chance."

Slater's answer was slowly and thoughtfully, even methodically, given. "Maybe. If the story ever gets up to the Marshal's office in Denver, which seems unlikely, there will have to be proof. Where will they get it? Not from you, Doctor. Not from John Holbrook. Not from his daughter. How about you, Mr. Templeton?"

"Not in a hundred years, Marshal."

"Satisfied, Doctor?"

Mailer leaned on the pole with clasped hands. "I'm not going to say you're not entitled to make this judgment, Marshal . . . I'm going to say I'm beholden to you, and I thank you."

Slater winked at Bart and gave Frank Mailer a light slap on the back. "You've got a gift; use it. . . . Now I've got to round up Kennedy, get Walt and Slim on their horses, round up a little help tying the other two on their saddles, and . . ." Slater suddenly paused. "On second thought I think I'll go talk to Mr. Holbrook. It'd be a lot better if he'd agree to bury them here on his ranch. That way they're out of sight—gone. There won't be questions asked like there would be if I hauled them over to Holtville." He winked again, turned on his heel, heading for the main house.

Jack Kennedy passed Marshal Slater near the main house. Neither one of them said a word. They nodded at each other, and Kennedy came down to the front of the barn where Dr. Mailer and Bart Templeton were standing.

"As far as I know, Doctor, Colorado doesn't want you for

anything you maybe did up north." Kennedy went to work rolling a smoke. "I'd like to get back to town. I don't like being away so long."

Bart said, "Slater's about ready to ride. He'll take Walt and Slim with him, and the bank loot."

Kennedy lighted his smoke and gazed at Bart with smoke trickling. "What about the other two?"

"He's going to see if John will bury them here on the ranch."

Kennedy considered Dr. Mailer. "What happens now, Doctor?"

Mailer was silent a long time, then he said, "I really don't know. I didn't expect it to end like this. I'll need some time to figure out what to do now."

Kennedy stood regarding the surgeon. "Well, we sure as hell need a doctor in the Blue Basin country. . . . John and I were talking in his bedroom. He owns six or seven buildings in Holtville. He's going to offer to give you clear title to any one of them you want if you'll agree to set up a doctorin' business down there. Think about it, Doctor. I'll promise you one thing: No one is going to come along and make trouble for you. I'll personally see to that. . . . I'd better go bring in the horses and start getting ready." Kennedy thrust out a big hand. "Doctor . . ."

Frank gripped Kennedy's hand, and afterward, as the big town marshal was entering the barn, Mailer turned to Bart. "Hell, I've got a choke in my throat I wouldn't even know how to diagnose. Bart, you—all you folks—I just can't believe running from the law can end like this. What can I say?"

Bart smiled. "Accept John's offer; set up a business down in Holtville. The next time I break something, I'll ride down and you can patch me up again."

Slater was emerging from the house with Nan Holbrook at the same time the *cocinero* came padding over from the cookshack. The old cook walked over to Mailer and said,

"Doctor, they tell me you worked wonders on Mr. Holbrook. . . . Listen, I wake up every morning with a damned headache." As he had been speaking, the cook had been gingerly probing the big bandage on his head. "Only thing that helps is a big cup of watered whiskey before breakfast."

Frank cast a sidelong glance at Bart, then said, "By all means, drink it if it stops the pain."

The cook's hangdog expression noticeably brightened because the scheme he'd devised before crossing the yard had succeeded so far without a hitch. "Well," he said, "it just ain't that easy," and now there was a whining hint to his voice. "You see, Mr. Holbrook's got this rule about no hired hands being allowed to have a bottle of whiskey on the ranch."

Frank and Bart exchanged amused looks before Mailer spoke again. "I'll speak to Mr. Holbrook for you. After all, a little watered whiskey once or twice a day never killed anyone that I know of."

The cook thanked him heartily and turned back in the direction of his cookshack.

Jack Kennedy came out of the barn and helped Slater load up the horses. They got Walt and Slim mounted on their saddled horses and tied their hands to the saddle horns. Slater and Kennedy mounted up. Slater looked at Frank Mailer and said, "Good luck, Doctor." Frank Kennedy smiled, too; then they rode out of the Holbrook yard leading the horses of their prisoners.

Frank Mailer was still watching the distant horsemen when he said to Bart, "If it had been a different U.S. marshal . . ."

Bart understood. "But it wasn't, Frank."

Mailer faintly nodded his head. "Would you call that predestination, Bart?"

"No. I'd call it justice the way justice is supposed to be, Frank. Now I've got to saddle up and head for home." Bart offered his left hand, and Frank Mailer squeezed it. As Bart walked away, Dr. Mailer started across the yard in the direction of the main house.

Bart was a mile out on his way home when he heard the cook ringing his triangle on the porch summoning the working crew to breakfast.

The big bay horse walked along enjoying both the sunshine and the exercise. Once, he swung his head to the left, held low, and bit the toe of the boot sticking partway through the stirrup. Not hard, just a nip. Bart laughed at him and leaned to pat his stud-neck.

They were friends.

When they reached the yard, though, those three colts out back did not welcome their return in a friendly manner. They had not been fed since the day before; they were both indignant and restless. They nickered and pawed, flung up their heads, and moved restlessly along the nearest side of their corral to the barn.

CHAPTER 23

Back to Normal

It was Saturday, three days after John Holbrook's surgery, before Bart saw a rider on his range. He was teaching the flashy chestnut horse figure eights about a mile from the yard when he saw the rider. It was Charley Lord, the range-boss.

"'Morning," Lord said when he rode up. "The way the weather's been the last few days makes it hard to believe how it was before that, eh?"

Bart nodded, and Charley studied the horse with the flaxen mane and tail. "Good-looking animal," he said, nodding his head in confirmation of his own opinion, then he said, "Things are going along pretty well at our place. Dr. Mailer took Mr. Holbrook up on his offer of a building down in Holtville. He rode down there yesterday and will look around and come back."

Bart was pleased about that. "How's Mr. Holbrook?"

"He still can't sit up in bed, but Nan says his appetite has returned."

Bart had another question. "What about those emigrants, Charley?"

"Well, that's where I was yesterday—up north along the

foothills making a horseback guess about where a hundred acres would be, and this mornin' I was going to go back and set some stakes when I saw you down here making figure eights. Thought I'd come on over because you haven't been back over to the yard since those lawmen left."

"Mr. Holbrook's goin' to let those folks settle up there?" Bart asked, and Charley nodded his head. "How is the little baby?"

"Looking fine and getting sassy." Charley sat gazing at the horse-breaker for a moment as though he had something on his mind. Finally, he said, "The Holbrooks would be pleased if you'd ride over, Bart. They want to thank you."

Bart returned the range-boss's gaze. "Maybe one of these days, Charley . . . I'm not real strong on that kind of talk."

The range-boss smiled. He understood. Gratitude was embarrassing. He raised his left hand with the reins in it. "Nice visiting with you." He turned away, set his horse into an easy lope, and went almost directly northward. The sun was still not very high, so he'd probably have time enough to reach the foothills, drive his stakes, and still get back to the Holbrook yard an hour or so before sundown.

Bart took the chestnut horse back, corralled him, and worked with another of the colts in the same corral. In the adjoining corral the big bay mustang watched everything with grave concern. He'd had two days to get the pleats out of his gut, and he had eaten his head off. Once, early in the morning, Bart had been in the barn when he heard a horse squeal. He stepped to the rear doorway.

The bay horse was doing everything by himself inside his corral he hadn't done while Bart had been on his back. He sunfished, bucked left and right, got his head down between his knees, and bawled in mock fury while he turned himself inside out.

Bart watched with keen interest. The bay horse bucked the way a real bucking horse did it; he sprang into the air

and when he came down his body was either far to the left
or the right as he humped up and kicked as hard as he could.
Then he spun, first in one direction then in another
direction. There was not a bronc rider on earth who could
have remained atop the big bay mustang.

When he was finished, the big horse stopped with his
head high, eyes bulging, nostrils distended, and let go with
a whistle that could have been heard a half mile away.

It was his way of letting off steam, of feeling so good he
had to do something violently physical. Afterward, he
gradually relaxed, his head came down a little, the hump
left his back, he eyed the man over in the barn doorway, and
eventually walked toward him as far as he could go, which
was to the pole gate.

Bart laughed and walked down to meet him, talking to
the horse. The bay did as the remount stallion did—put his
head down and half closed his eyes as the two-legged
creature scratched his mane and stroked his forehead.

To the horse-breaker it had always been worth a lot of
money to have an animal offer his faith and trust this way.
Not all horses did it, even a great many horses who lost their
fear of two-legged creatures did not do it. Nor could it be
induced; it was something a horse had to come to by
himself.

The following day was Sunday. Bart rode the bay horse in
the morning. They made a sashay around the southwestern
range looking for Big Ben and his harem. They did not find
them, so they spent the afternoon riding north and eastward.

They found the loose stock up where they had encountered them in the identical bosquet of trees the day Bart had
seen smoke and had found the emigrant camp.

The remount stallion came out to offer battle, then he
hesitated, for although he recognized the big bay horse as
the one that had left him lying senseless after their last
meeting, there was something different. The big bay horse
no longer smelled like a studhorse.

Big Ben came ahead with mincing steps and an arched neck. The big bay horse watched him. Gelded or not, he would fight. But Big Ben wanted to verify the smell and that was all. He sidled in close to stretch his neck as far as he could and wrinkle his nose. He did that several times before being reassured, then he stood back.

Bart laughed at him and rode on through the mares and colts, and as before, the oldest colts fled in mock terror, heads and tails up, only to make a mile-wide circle, then return to the side of their dams.

There was a horseman a fair distance eastward, and because Bart was sure it was Charley Lord, he headed toward him.

Charley raised an arm, and Bart waved back. Bart's curiosity was aroused. They'd talked casually earlier in the day. If Charley'd had anything important to tell him, it seemed that he would have said it at their former meeting. Bart speculated that after Charley had returned to the Holbrook yard something had come up to require him to saddle up and ride back. "I got a message for you," Lord said.

Bart leaned and nodded his head but said nothing.

"You know Simon Butler who rides for us?"

Bart knew Butler. He was the horse-breaker for John Holbrook. He had never been greatly impressed by Simon's ability with horses. "Yeah, what about him?"

"He quit to take a job with the blacksmith down in Holtville. Mr. Holbrook sent me over to ask if you'd be willing to take Simon's place."

Bart eyed the tall, lean man thoughtfully. He said, "Charley, I can't do that. I've got horses to break, my own place to look after. Besides, I'm out of practice working for other people. I've been my own boss four years now. It's a good feeling."

The range-boss was sympathetic. "I told him something

like that would be your answer. He told me to come over and ask you anyway."

"Why does he want to do that? Charley, he doesn't owe me anything, if that's what's bothering him. Hell, you can find another horse-breaker."

The range-boss gazed steadily at Bart with a hint of a faint smile around his lips. "Do me a favor, Bart. Ride over tomorrow and tell him your answer. Mr. Holbrook is flat on his belly in that damned bed. He's restless as a kitten in a box of shavings. Ride over and set a spell with him." The range-boss turned his horse toward home and looked over his shoulder at Bart. "I'll tell him you'll be over in the morning. All right?"

Bart had the feeling that there was more to this than there appeared to be, so he said, "Charley, just what the hell is this all about?"

The range-boss's eyes twinkled. "We need someone to take the snap out of some big colts. I got an idea that if you'd just agree to handle the colts, it'd be fine with Mr. Holbrook if you brought them over here to do it. You'd be getting paid for doin' something you do every day anyway, on your own place and you being your own boss. . . . Try that on him tomorrow, Bart."

The range-boss nodded and rode eastward. The sun was down, but this time of year daylight would linger for another couple of hours.

CHAPTER 24

Return of the Sun

It was another beautiful day when Bart saddled the big bay horse, put a squaw bridle on the flashy chestnut gelding, and left the yard riding one and leading one.

He was not enthusiastic about any part of this visit except when he would hand Nan Holbrook the lead-rope of the chestnut horse as he'd promised. He remembered her reluctance when he'd mentioned giving her the horse, but that had been a bad storm, four outlaws, and two dead men ago.

By the time he reached the Holbrook yard the sun was climbing. Bart swung off and tied both horses in front of the barn.

Bart got to the steps leading to the veranda of the main house before the door opened and Nan stepped out booted for riding. She smiled at him. "Good morning. It's been a week, Bart."

He walked closer to her. She looked particularly beautiful in a cream-colored blouse and a divided riding skirt of split buckskin. Her shining black hair matched the luster of her dark eyes. "Good morning. You look pretty as a picture."

He had not said that intentionally—it simply came out

because that was what he was thinking. But it embarrassed
him, so he also said, "How is your pa?"

She stepped back for him to enter the parlor, then took
him through the house to her father's bedroom. John
Holbrook still could not lie on his back, but he had devised
a way of propping his head so that he could see people in the
room fairly well.

Nan pointed to a chair near the head of the bed, and Bart
sat on it. Nan's father looked steadily at him for a moment
before saying, "Charley said you didn't want Simon's job."

Bart turned his hat in his hands. "I'll do this for you,
John. I'll break colts but only over at my place, where I've
got everything set up for handling them."

Holbrook glanced around at his daughter, who was
standing between his bed and Bart's chair. But he said
nothing until he faced Bart again. "All right. Over at your
place. But I want to send one of my riders over to lend a
hand."

Bart began to faintly frown. He did not need an assistant
and had never worked with one. Horse-breaking was a one-
man job.

John Holbrook jerked his head slightly and said, "Her."

Bart raised his eyes to Nan's face. She did not look at
him; she looked at her father. Bart began turning the old hat
he was holding between this knees again. He did not want to
refuse, not in front of Holbrook's daughter, but he did not
particularly want her getting in his way, either. He shot a
look out the far window tring to think of a tactful way of
getting out of this situation.

John Holbrook did not allow him time enough to devise a
way. "We have four head Simon broke to lead, but that's all
they know. I'll have Charley and another man or two take
them over to your corrals in the morning. Bart, is fifteen
dollars a head all right?"

Fifteen dollars to break a green colt was more than most
people paid by half. He nodded dumbly.

Holbrook smiled. "She's good with horses, Bart."

Bart nodded about that too.

Holbrook closed his eyes; Nan tapped Bart on the shoulder and led him out of the room. As the two walked through the doorway, Holbrook stealthily watched them before closing his eyes again to rest.

Bart did not say a word until they were down in front of the barn, then he untied the chestnut horse and handed it to her. "Yours," he told her.

She stared at him. "I can't accept him."

"Why not? I want you to have him."

She looked past at the handsome horse. "Did you know that mothers warn their daughters never to accept gifts from men?"

He did not know this.

She said, "My mother told me never to accept a horse as a gift from a man unless I was prepared to marry him. That was the only time an Indian offered a woman a horse."

He frowned at her. "I'm not an Indian."

She smiled. "I'm half-Indian." She watched shadows of troubled thought pass across his bronzed features. She was waiting for the question her remark had invited, but he did not ask it.

Instead, he said, "Ride him, Nan. You'll fall in love with him."

She considered the horse again. "All right. I'll saddle, and we can ride out a ways." She smiled sweetly at him before going down into the barn for her saddle, blanket, and bridle.

They left the yard riding northward. As they passed the wagon shed north of the barn, Bart noticed the vacant place where the emigrant wagon had been parked. Nan saw his look and said, "The Wiltons drove back to the foothills yesterday, after Charley marked their hundred acres and my father promised to have it surveyed so he could give them a deed to it."

Bart smiled at her. "That made them happy, eh?"

She smiled back. "Like a pair of children. I like them, Bart."

The chestnut horse went along quietly and tractably. He had an easy gait. Nan set their course slightly eastward in the direction of a stand of trees several miles away. She patted the horse's neck and said, "You were right—I'm falling in love with him."

Bart beamed.

"But I still can't accept him." She dismounted and stood beside the chestnut.

"Nan . . ."

"Yes, Bart.'

". . . Nothing." He swung down and took the reins of both horses.

She did not take her eyes off him. "What is it? Bart, whatever it is, I'll understand."

"Well, if I was an Indian and offered him to you . . . ?"

She smiled softly at him. "I'd accept him."

"Well, hell, right this minute I'd sure like to be an Indian."

"You don't have to be an Indian, Bart."

He looked at the chestnut horse, then around through this shady place, and finally back to her. "You know what I am and what I have—not much on both counts. That chestnut horse is the best I can offer you, Nan."

"No, it's not," she told him.

"Well . . . I'll tell you something. I've thought a lot about you over the years, but it was impossible, and until today I never thought I'd tell you this: I'm in love with you."

Her black eyes turned misty; she only hesitated a moment then threw her arms around him. He dropped the reins and held her awkwardly until the surprise passed, then his arms tightened. He quietly said, "Your pa will shot me."

Her voice sounded muffled against his chest. "My father knows."

His grip loosened a little. "Knows what?"

"That I've been in love with you for a long time. Yesterday we talked about it. His idea of getting you over here to break horses for us was clumsy, I know, but he insisted on sending Charley over to ask you. I told him it wouldn't work . . ." She pulled back slightly and looked up into his face. "He needs me until he can walk, Bart. That was his solution to two problems: getting you over here and not losing me."

He kissed her with an intensity that surprised him. They were interrupted by the sound of the bay horse lustily clearing its nostrils.

Bart gazed at the chestnut horse over Nan's shoulder. He said, "I don't think I'll ever give another horse to a woman."

She looked up at him. "Not if you know what's good for you, you won't," and they laughed.

When Bart and Nan rode back toward the yard, he said, "Are you going to tell your pa I gave you the chestnut horse?"

She nodded and shot him a quick look of understanding. "You're wondering what he'll say?"

"Yes."

"Bart, that's how he proposed to my mother."

At the barn they cared for their animals, then went directly to the main house. Nan lighted a couple of lamps and took one to her father's room. Bart lingered in the doorway, believing her father was asleep.

He wasn't. John Holbrook watched her put the lamp on a little table, then raised his eyes to her face, read all he had to know from the radiance of her expression. He twisted his neck as far as he could so that he could also see Bart, and said, "It's all settled between you two?"

Bart walked closer so Holbrook would not have to strain

to see him. He had a twinkle in his eyes as he said, "I offered her a nice chestnut gelding with a flaxen mane and tail."

Holbrook looked at Bart. "And she accepted it?"

"Yes."

Nan slipped past Bart to the side of the bed and leaned to be kissed by her father. There were tears on her cheeks as she moved back. Bart stepped up. Holbrook said, "Take my hand," and Bart obeyed. Holbrook squeezed, and Bart squeezed back.

Outside, the *cocinero* began beating his triangle, summoning the riders to supper. Nan left the two men, heading for the kitchen to supper.

Bart sat down on the bedside chair. "That hired hand you offered to have help me with the colts; I'll accept the offer too."

They grinned at each other as dusk began to settle across the yard.

About the Author

Lauran Paine lives in Greenview, California. He is an accomplished western writer who has published dozens of books under various pseudonyms and his own name.

Tales of the West by T.V. OLSEN

JUL -- 2020